Bones

Other Titles include:
Edgar Wallace, *Sanders of the River*
John Galsworthy, *Uncollected Forsyte*
Joseph Conrad, *The Rover*
Arthur Conan Doyle, *The Great Shadow*
Edgar Wallace, *The People of the River*
Edgar Wallace, *Bones*
Edgar Wallace, *Bosambo of the River*
Herbert Jenkins, *Bindle*

This edition of *Bones*
first published 1987 by Greenhill Books,
Lionel Leventhal Limited, 3 Barham Avenue,
Elstree, Hertfordshire WD6 3PW

This edition © Lionel Leventhal Limited, 1987

British Library Cataloguing in Publication Data
Wallace, Edgar
Bones: A "Sanders of the River" book. –
(Greenhill Famous Authors)
I. Title. 823'.912 [F] PR6045.A327

ISBN 0-947898-71-9 ✓

Publishing History
Bones was first published in 1915 and this edition
is complete and unabridged. In reproducing this work
there are a few cases of language being used which
may have changed its meaning over the years or which
is less acceptable today than it was at the turn of
the century, and would not be used in a newly-written book.

For information about Edgar Wallace write to
The Edgar Wallace Society,
7 Devonshire Close, Amersham, Bucks HP6 5JG.

Greenhill Books
welcome readers' suggestions for books that might be
added to this Series. Please write to us if there are
titles which you would like to recommend.

Printed by Antony Rowe Limited,
Chippenham, Wiltshire.

EDGAR WALLACE

Bones

A "Sanders of the River" book

GREENHILL
FAMOUS
AUTHORS

CONTENTS

YOU will never know from the perusal of the Blue Book the true inwardness of the happenings in the Ochori country in the spring of the year of Wish. Nor all the facts associated with the disappearance of the Rt. Hon. Joseph Blowter, Secretary of State for the Colonies.

We know (though this is not in the Blue Books) that Bosambo called together all his petty chiefs and his headmen, from one end of the country to the other, and assembled them squatting expectantly at the foot of the little hillock, where sat Bosambo in his robes of office (unauthorised but no less magnificent), their upturned faces charged with pride and confidence, eloquent of the hold this sometime Liberian convict had upon the wayward and fearful folk of the Ochori.

Now no man may call a palaver of all small chiefs unless he notifies the government of his intention, for the government is jealous of self-appointed parliaments, for when men meet together in public conference, however innocent may be its first cause, talk invariably drifts to war, just as when they assemble and talk in private it drifts womanward.

And since a million and odd square miles of territory may only be governed by a handful of ragged soldiers so long as there is no concerted action against authority, extemporised and spontaneous palavers are severely discouraged.

But Bosambo was too cheery and optimistic a man to doubt that his action would incur the censorship of his lord, and, moreover, he was so filled with his own high plans and so warm and generous at heart at the thought of the benefits he might be conferring upon his patron that the illegality of the meeting did not occur to him, or if it occurred was dismissed as too preposterous for consideration.

And so there had come by the forest paths, by canoe, from fishing villages, from far-off agricultural lands near by the great mountains, from timber cuttings in the lower forest, higher chiefs and little chiefs, headmen and lesser headmen, till they made a respectable crowd, too vast for the comfort of the Ochori elders who must needs provide them with food and lodgings.

"Noble chiefs of the Ochori," began Bosambo, and Notiki nudged his neighbour with a sharp elbow, for Notiki was an old man of forty-three, and thin.

"Our lord desires us to give him something," he said.

He was a bitter man this Notiki, a relative of former chiefs of the Ochori, and now no more than over-head of four villages.

"Wa!" said his neighbour, with his shining face turned to Bosambo.

Notiki grunted but said no more.

"I have assembled you here," said Bosambo, "because I love to see you, and because it is good that I should meet those who are in authority under me to administer the laws which the King my master has set for your guidance."

Word for word it was a paraphrase of an address which Sanders himself had delivered three months ago. His audience may have forgotten the fact, but Notiki at least recognised the plagiarism and said "Oh, ho!" under his breath and made a scornful noise.

"Now I must go from you," said Bosambo.

There was a little chorus of dismay, but Notiki's voice did not swell the volume.

"The King has called me to the coast, and for the space of two moons I shall be as dead to you, though my fetish will watch you and my spirit will walk these streets every night with big ears to listen to evil talk, and great big eyes to see the hearts of men. Yea, from this city to the very end of my dominions over to Kalala." His accusing eyes fixed Notiki, and the thin man wriggled uncomfortably.

8

"This man is a devil," he muttered under his breath, "he hears and sees all things."

"And if you ask me why I go," Bosambo went on, "I tell you this: swearing you all to secrecy that this word shall not go beyond your huts" (there was some two thousand people present to share the mystery), "my lord Sandi has great need of me. For who of us is so wise that he can look into the heart and understand the sorrow-call which goes from brother to brother and from blood to blood. I say no more save my lord desires me, and since I am the King of the Ochori, a nation great amongst all nations, must I go down to the coast like a dog or like the headman of a fisher-village?"

He paused dramatically, and there was a faint—a very faint—murmur which he might interpret as an expression of his people's wish that he should travel in a state bordering upon magnificence.

Faint indeed was that murmur, because there was a hint of taxation in the business, a promise of levies to be extracted from an unwilling peasantry; a suggestion of lazy men leaving the comfortable shade of their huts to hurry perspiring in the forest that gum and rubber and similar offerings should be laid at the complacent feet of their overlord.

Bosambo heard the murmur and marked its horrid lack of heartiness and was in no sense put out of countenance.

"As you say," said he approvingly, "it is proper that I should journey to my lord and to the strange people beyond the coast—to the land where even slaves wear trousers—carrying with me most wonderful presents that the name of the Ochori shall be as thunder upon the waters and even great kings shall speak in pride of you." He paused again.

Now it was a dead silence which greeted his peroration. Notably unenthusiastic was this gathering, twiddling its toes and blandly avoiding his eye. Two moons before he had extracted something more than his tribute—a tribute which was the prerogative of government.

Yet then, as Notiki said under his breath, or openly, or by innuendo as the sentiment of his company demanded, four and twenty canoes laden with the fruits of taxation had come to the Ochori city, and five only of those partly filled had paddled down to headquarters to carry the Ochori tribute to the overlord of the land.

"I will bring back with me new things," said Bosambo enticingly; "strange devil boxes, large magics which will entrance you, things that no common man has seen, such as I and Sandi alone know in all this land. Go now, I tell thee, to your people in this country, telling them all that I have spoken to you, and when the moon is in a certain quarter they will come in joy bearing presents in both hands, and these ye shall bring to me."

"But, lord!" it was the bold Notiki who stood in protest, "what shall happen to such of us headmen who come without gifts in our hands for your lordship, saying 'Our people are stubborn and will give nothing'?"

"Who knows?" was all the satisfaction he got from Bosambo, with the additional significant hint, "I shall not blame you, knowing that it is not because of your fault but because your people do not love you, and because they desire another chief over them. The palaver is finished."

Finished it was, so far as Bosambo was concerned. He called a council of his headmen that night in his hut.

Bosambo made his preparations at leisure. There was much to avoid before he took his temporary farewell of the tribe. Not the least to be counted amongst those things to be done was the extraction, to its uttermost possibility, of the levy which he had quite improperly instituted.

And of the things to avoid, none was more urgent or called for greater thought than the necessity for so timing his movements that he did not come upon Sanders or drift within the range of his visible and audible influence.

Here fortune may have been with Bosambo, but it is more

likely that he had carefully thought out every detail of his scheme. Sanders at the moment was collecting hut tax along the Kisai river and there was also, as Bosambo well knew, a murder trial of great complexity waiting for his decision at Ikan. A headman was suspected of murdering his chief wife, and the only evidence against him was that of the under wives to whom she displayed much hauteur and arrogance.

The people of the Ochori might be shocked at the exorbitant demands which their lord put upon them, but they were too wise to deny him his wishes. There had been a time in the history of the Ochori when demands were far heavier, and made with great insolence by a people who bore the reputation of being immensely fearful. It had come to be a by-word of the people when they discussed their lord with greater freedom than he could have wished, the tyranny of Bosambo was better than the tyranny of Akasava.

Amongst the Ochori chiefs, greater and lesser, only one was conspicuous by his failure to carry proper offerings to his lord. When all the gifts were laid on sheets of native cloth in the great space before Bosambo's hut, Notiki's sheet was missing and with good reason as he sent his son to explain.

"Lord," said this youth, lank and wild, "my father has collected for you many beautiful things, such as gum and rubber and the teeth of elephants. Now he would have brought these and laid them at your lovely feet, but the roads through the forest are very evil, and there have been floods in the northern country and he cannot pass the streams. Also the paths through the forest are thick and tangled and my father fears for his carriers."

Bosambo looked at him, thoughtfully.

"Go back to your father, N'gobi," he said gently, "and tell him that though there come no presents from him to me, I, his master and chief, knowing he loves me, understand all things well."

N'gobi brightened visibly. He had been ready to bolt,

understanding something of Bosambo's dexterity with a stick and fearing that the chief would loose upon him the vengeance his father had called down upon his own hoary head.

"Of the evil roads I know," said Bosambo; "now this you shall say to your father: Bosambo the chief goes away from this city and upon a long journey; for two moons he will be away doing the business of his cousin and friend Sandi. And when my lord Bim-bi has bitten once at the third moon I will come back and I will visit your father. But because the roads are bad," he went on, "and the floods come even in this dry season," he said significantly, "and the forest is so entangled that he cannot bring his presents, sending only the son of his wife to me, he shall make against my coming such a road as shall be in width, the distance between the King's hut and the hut of the King's wife; and he shall clear from this road all there are of trees, and he shall bridge the strong stream and dig pits for the floods. And to this end he shall take every man of his kingdom and set them to labour, and as they work they shall sing a song which goes:

We are doing Notiki's work,
The work Notiki set us to do,
Rather than send to the lord his King
The presents which Bosambo demanded.

The palaver is finished."

This is the history, or the beginning of the history, of the straight road which cuts through the heart of the Ochori country from the edge of the river by the cataracts, even to the mountains of the great King, a road famous throughout Africa and imperishably associated with Bosambo's name— this by the way.

On the first day following the tax palaver Bosambo went down the river with four canoes, each canoe painted beautifully with camwood and gum, and with twenty-four paddlers.

It was by a fluke that he missed Sanders. As it happened, the Commissioner had come back to the big river to collect the evidence of the murdered woman's brother who was a petty headman of an Isisi fishing village. The *Zaire* came into the river almost as the last of Bosambo's canoes went round the bend out of sight, and since a legend existed on the river, a legend for the inception of which Bosambo himself was mainly responsible, that he was in some way related to Mr. Commissioner Sanders, no man spoke of Bosambo's passing.

The chief came to headquarters on the third day after his departure from his city. His subsequent movements are somewhat obscure, even to Sanders, who has been at some pains to trace them.

It is known that he drew a hundred and fifty pounds in English gold from Sanders' storekeeper—he had piled up a fairly extensive credit during the years of his office—that he embarked with one headman and his wife on a coasting boat due for Sierra Leone, and that from that city came a long-winded demand in Arabic by a ragged messenger for a further instalment of one hundred pounds. Sanders heard the news on his return to headquarters and was a little worried.

" I wonder if the devil is going to desert his people?" he said.

Hamilton the Houssa laughed.

"He is more likely to desert his people than to desert a balance of four hundred pounds which now stands to his credit here," he said. "Bosambo has felt the call of civilisation. I suppose he ought to have secured your permission to leave his territory?"

"He has given his people work to keep them busy," Sanders said a little gravely. "I have had a passionate protest from Notiki, one of his chiefs in the north. Bosambo has set him to build a road through the forest, and Notiki objects."

The two men were walking across the yellow parade ground past the Houssas hut in the direction of headquarters' bungalow.

"What about your murderer?" asked Hamilton, after a

while, as they mounted the broad wooden steps which led to the bungalow stoep.

Sanders shook his head.

"Everybody lied," he said briefly. "I can do no less than send the man to the Village. I could have hung him on clear evidence, but the lady seemed to have been rather unpopular and the murderer quite a person to be commended in the eyes of the public. The devil of it is," he said as he sank into his big chair with a sigh, "that had I hanged him it would not have been necessary to write three fóolscap sheets of report. I dislike these domestic murderers intensely—give me a ravaging brigand with the hands of all people against him."

"You'll have one if you don't touch wood," said Hamilton seriously.

Hamilton came of Scottish stock—and the Scots are notorious prophets.

II

Now the truth may be told of Bosambo, and all his movements may be explained by this revelation of his benevolence. In the silence of his hut had he planned his schemes. In the dark aisles of the forests, under starless skies when his fellow-huntsmen lay deep in the sleep which the innocent and the barbarian alone enjoy; in drowsy moments when he sat dispensing justice, what time litigants had droned monotonously he had perfected his scheme.

Imagination is the first fruit of civilisation and when the reverend fathers of the coast taught Bosambo certain magics, they were also implanting in him the ability to picture possibilities, and shape from his knowledge of human affairs the eventual consequences of his actions. This is imagination somewhat elaborately and clumsily defined.

To one person only had Bosambo unburdened himself of his schemes.

14

In the privacy of his great hut he had sat with his wife, a steaming dish of fish between them, for however lax Bosambo might be, his wife was an earnest follower of the Prophet and would tolerate no such abomination as the flesh of the cloven-hoofed goat.

He had told her many things.

"Light of my heart," said he, "our lord Sandi is my father and my mother, a giver of riches, and a plentiful provider of pence. Now it seems to me, that though he is a just man and great, having neither fear of his enemies nor soft words for his friends, yet the lords of his land who live so very far away do him no honour."

"Master," said the woman quietly, "is it no honour that he should be placed as a king over us?"

Bosambo beamed approvingly.

"Thou hast spoken the truth, oh my beloved!" said he, in the extravagance of his admiration. "Yet I know much of the white folk, for I have lived along this coast from Dacca to Mossomedes. Also I have sailed to a far place called Madagascar, which is on the other side of the world, and I know the way of white folk. Even in Benguella there is a governor who is not so great as Sandi, and about his breast are all manner of shining stars that glitter most beautifully in the sun, and he wears ribbons about him and bright-coloured sashes and swords." He wagged his finger impressively. "Have I not said that he is not so great as Sandi. When saw you my lord with stars or cross or sash or a sword?"

"Also at Decca, where the Frenchy live. At certain places in the Togo, which is Allamandi,[1] I have seen men with this same style of ornaments, for thus it is that the white folk do honour to their kind."

He was silent a long time and his brown-eyed wife looked at him curiously.

[1] Allamandi—German territory.

15

"Yet what can you do, my lord?" she asked. "Although you are very powerful, and Sandi loves you, this is certain, that none will listen to *you* and do honour to Sandi at your word—though I do not know the ways of the white people, yet of this I am sure."

Again Bosambo's large mouth stretched from ear to ear, and his two rows of white teeth gleamed pleasantly.

"You are as the voice of wisdom and the very soul of cleverness," he said, "for you speak that which is true. Yet I know ways, for I am very cunning and wise, being a holy man and acquainted with blessed apostles such as Paul and the blessed Peter, who had his ear cut off because a certain dancing woman desired it. Also by magic it was put on again because he could not hear the cocks crow. All this and similar things I have here." He touched his forehead.

Wise woman that she was, she had made no attempt to pry into her husband's business, but spent the days preparing for the journey, she and the nut-brown sprawling child of immense girth, who was the apple of Bosambo's eye.

So Bosambo had passed down the river as has been described, and four days after he left there disappeared from the Ochori village ten brothers in blood of his, young hunting men who had faced all forms of death for the very love of it, and these vanished from the land and none knew where they went save that they did not follow on their master's trail.

Tukili, the chief of the powerful eastern island Isisi, or, as it is contemptuously called, the N'gombi-Isisi, by the riverain folk, went hunting one day, and ill-fortune led him to the border of the Ochori country. Ill fortune was it for one Fimili, a straight maid of fourteen, beautiful by native standard, who was in the forest searching for roots which were notorious as a cure for "boils" which distressed her unamiable father.

Tukili saw the girl and desired her, and that which Tukili desired he took. She offered little opposition to being

16

carried away to the Isisi city when she discovered that her life would be spared, and possibly was no worse off in the harem of Tukili than she would have been in the hut of the poor fisherman for whom her father had designed her. A few years before, such an incident would have passed almost unnoticed.

The Ochori were so used to being robbed of women and of goats, so meek in their acceptance of wrongs that would have set the spears of any other nation shining, that they would have accepted the degradation and preserved a sense of thankfulness that the robber had limited his raiding to one girl, and that a maid. But with the coming of Bosambo there had arrived a new spirit in the Ochori. They had learnt their strength, incidentally they had learnt their rights. The father of the girl went hot-foot to his over-chief, Notiki, and covered himself with ashes at the door of the chief's hut.

"This is a bad palaver," said Notiki, "and since Bosambo has deserted us and is making our marrows like water that we should build him a road, and there is none in this land whom I may call chief or who may speak with authority, it seems by my age and by relationship to the kings of this land, I must do that which is desirable."

So he gathered together two thousand men who were working on the road and were very pleased indeed to carry something lighter than rocks and felled trees, and with these spears he marched into the Isisi forest, burning and slaying whenever he came upon a little village which offered no opposition. Thus he took to himself the air and title of conqueror with as little excuse as a flamboyant general ever had.

Had it occurred on the river, this warlike expedition must have attracted the attention of Sanders. The natural roadway of the territory is a waterway. It is only when operations are begun against the internal tribes who inhabit the bush, and whose armies can move under the cloak of the forest (and none wiser) that Sanders found himself at a disadvantage.

Tukili himself heard nothing of the army that was being led against him until it was within a day's march of his gates. Then he sallied forth with a force skilled in warfare and practised in the hunt. The combat lasted exactly ten minutes and all that was left of Notiki's spears made the best of their way homeward, avoiding, as far as possible, those villages which they had visited en route with such disastrous results to the unfortunate inhabitants.

Now it is impossible that one conqueror shall be sunk to oblivion without his victor claiming for himself the style of his victim. Tukili had defeated his adversary, and Tukili was no exception to the general rule, and from being a fairly well-disposed king, amiable—too amiable as we have shown —and kindly, and just, he became of a sudden a menace to all that part of Sanders' territory which lies between the French land and the river.

It was such a situation as this as only Bosambo might deal with, and Sanders heartily cursed his absent chief and might have cursed him with greater fervour had he an inkling of the mission to which Bosambo had appointed himself.

III

His Excellency the Administrator of the period had his office at a prosperous city of stone which we will call Koombooli, though that is not its name.

He was a stout, florid man, patient and knowledgeable. He had been sent to clear up the mess which two incompetent administrators made, who had owed their position rather to the constant appearance of their friends and patrons in the division lobbies than to their acquaintance with the native mind, and it is eloquent of the regard in which His Excellency was held that, although he was a Knight

18

Commander of St. Michael and St. George, a Companion of a Victorian Order, a Commander of the Bath, and the son of a noble house, he was known familiarly along the coast to all administrators, commissioners, even to the deputy inspectors, as " Bob ".

Bosambo came to the presence with an inward quaking. In a sense he had absconded from his trust, and he did not doubt that Sanders had made all men acquainted with the suddenness and the suspicious character of his disappearance.

And the first words of His Excellency the Administrator confirmed all Bosambo's worst fears.

" O chief! " said Sir Robert with a little twinkle in his eye. " Are you so fearful of your people that you run away from them? "

" Mighty master, " answered Bosambo, humbly, " I do not know fear, for as your honour may have heard, I am a very brave man, fearing nothing save my lord Sanders' displeasure. "

A ghost of a smile played about the corners of Sir Robert's mouth.

" That you have earned, my friend, " said he. " Now you shall tell me why you came away secretly, also why you desired this palaver with me. And do not lie, Bosambo, " he said, " for I am he who hung three chiefs on Gallows Hill above Grand Bassam because they spoke falsely. "

This was one of the fictions which was current on the coast, and was implicitly believed in by the native population. The truth will be recounted at another time, but it is sufficient to say that Bosambo was one of those who did not doubt the authenticity of the legend.

" Now I will speak to you, O my lord, " he said earnestly, " and I speak by all oaths, both the oaths of my own people——"

" Spare me the oaths of the Kroo folk, " protested Sir Robert, and raised a warning hand.

" Then by Markie and Lukie will I swear, " said Bosambo,

fervently; "those fine fellows of whom Your Excellency knows. I have sat long in the country of the Ochori, and I have ruled wisely according to my abilities. And over me at all times was Sandi, who was a father to his people and so beautiful of mind and countenance that when he came to us even the dead folk would rise up to speak to him. This is a miracle," said Bosambo profoundly but cautiously, "which I have heard but which I have not seen. Now this I ask you who see all things, and here is the puzzle which I will set to your honour. If Sandi is so great and so wise, and is so loved by the greater King, how comes it that he stays for ever in one place, having no beautiful stars about his neck nor wonderful ribbons around his stomach such as the great Frenchiman—and the great Allamandi men, and even the Portuguesi men wear who are honoured by their kings?"

It was a staggering question, and Sir Robert Sanleigh sat up and stared at the solemn face of the man before him.

Bosambo, an unromantic figure in trousers, jacket, and shirt—he was collarless—had thrust his hands deeply into unaccustomed pockets, ignorant of the disrespect which such an attitude displayed, and was staring back at the Administrator.

"O chief!" asked the puzzled Sir Robert, "this is a strange palaver you make—who gave you these ideas?"

"Lord, none gave me this idea save my own bright mind," said Bosambo. "Yes, many nights have I laid thinking of these things for I am just and I have faith."

His Excellency kept his unwavering eye upon the other. He had heard of Bosambo, knew him as an original, and at this moment was satisfied in his own mind of the other's sincerity.

A smaller man than he, his predecessor for example, might have dismissed the preposterous question as an impertinence and given the questioner short shrift. But Sir Robert understood his native.

"These are things too high for me, Bosambo," he said.

"What dog am I that I should question the mind of my lords? In their wisdom they give honour and they punish. It is written."

Bosambo nodded.

"Yet, lord," he persisted, "my own cousin who sweeps your lordship's stables told me this morning that on the days of big palavers you also have stars and beautiful things upon your breast, and noble ribbons about your lordship's stomach. Now your honour shall tell me by whose favour these things come about."

Sir Robert chuckled.

"Bosambo," he said solemnly, "they gave these things to me because I am an old man. Now when your lord Sandi becomes old these honours also will he receive."

He saw Bosambo's face fall and went on:

"Also much may happen that will bring Sandi to their lordships' eyes, they who sit above us. Some great deed that he may do, some high service he may offer to his king. All these happenings bring nobility and honour. Now," he went on kindly, "go back to your people, remembering that I shall think of you and of Sandi, and that I shall know that you came because of your love for him, and that on a day which is written I will send a book to my masters speaking well of Sandi, for his sake and for the sake of the people who love him. The palaver is finished."

Bosambo went out of the Presence a dissatisfied man, passed through the hall where a dozen commissioners and petty chiefs were waiting audience, skirted the great white building and came in time to his own cousin, who swept the stables of His Excellency the Administrator. And here, in the coolness of the stone-walled mews, he learnt much about the Administrator; little tit-bits of information which were unlikely to be published in the official gazette. Also he acquired a considerable amount of data concerning the giving of honours, and after a long examination and cross-examination of his wearied relative he left him as dry as a sucked orange, but happy in the possession of a new five-shilling piece which Bosambo had magnificently pressed upon him, and which subsequently proved to be bad.

IV

By the River of Spirits is a deep forest which stretches back and back in a dense and chaotic tangle of strangled sapling and parasitic weed to the edge of the Pigmy forest. No man—white or brown or black—has explored the depth of the Forbidden Forest, for here the wild beasts have their lairs and rear their young; and here are mosquito in dense clouds. Moreover, and this is important, a certain potent ghost named Bim-bi stalks restlessly from one border of the forest to the other. Bim-bi is older than the sun and more terrible than any other ghost. For he feeds on the moon, and at nights you may see how the edge of the desert world is bitten by his great mouth until it becomes, first, the half of a moon, then the merest slither, and then no moon at all. And on the very dark nights, when the gods are hastily making him a new meal, the ravenous Bim-bi calls to his need the stars; and you may watch, as every little boy of the Akasava has watched, clutching his father's hand tightly in his fear, the hot rush of meteors across the velvet sky to the rapacious and open jaws of Bim-bi.

He was a ghost respected by all peoples—Akasava, Ochori, Isisi, N'gombi, and Bush folk. By the Bolengi, the Bomongo, and even the distant Upper Congo people feared him. Also all the chiefs for generations upon generations had sent tribute of corn and salt to the edge of the forest for his propitiation, and it is a legend that when the Isisi fought the Akasava in the great war, the envoy of the Isisi was admitted without molestation to the enemy's lines in order to lay an offering at Bim-bi's feet. Only one man in the world, so far as the People of the River know, has ever spoken slightingly of Bim-bi, and that man was Bosambo of the Ochori, who had no respect for any ghosts save of his own creation.

It is the custom of the Akasava district to hold a ghost palaver to which the learned men of all tribes are invited, and the palaver takes place in the village of Ookos by the edge of the forest.

On a certain day in the year of the floods and when Bosambo was gone a month from his land, there came messengers chance-found and walking in terror to all the principal cities and villages of the Akasava, of the Isisi, and of the N'gombi-Isisi carrying this message:

"Mimbimi, son of Simbo Sako, son of Ogi, has opened his house to his friends on the night when Bim-bi has swallowed the moon."

A summons to such a palaver in the second name of Bim-bi was not one likely to be ignored, but a summons from Mimbimi was at least to be wondered at and to be speculated upon, for Mimbimi was an unknown quantity, though some gossips professed to know him as the chief of one of the Nomadic tribes which ranged the heart of the forest, preying on Akasava and Isisi with equal discrimination. But these gossips were of a mind not peculiar to any nationality or to any colour. They were those jealous souls who either could not or would not confess that they were ignorant on the topic of the moment.

Be he robber chief, or established by law and government, this much was certain. Mimbimi had called for his secret palaver and the most noble and arrogant of chiefs must obey, even though the obedience spelt disaster for the daring man who had summoned them to conference.

Tuligini, a victorious captain, not lightly to be summoned, might have ignored the invitation but for the seriousness of his elder men, who, versed in the conventions of Bim-bi and those who invoked his name, stood aghast at the mere suggestion that this palaver should be ignored. Tuligini demanded, and with reason:

"Who was this who dare call the vanquished of Bosambo to a palaver? for am I not the great buffalo of the forest? and do not all men bow down to me in fear?"

"Lord, you speak the truth," said his trembling councillor, "yet this is a ghost palaver and all manner of evils come to those who do not obey."

Sanders, through his spies, heard of the summons in the name of Bim-bi, and was a little troubled. There was nothing too small to be serious in the land over which he ruled.

As for instance: Some doubt existed in the Lesser N'gombi country as to whether teeth filed to a point were more becoming than teeth left as Nature placed them. Tombini, the chief of N'gombi, held the view that Nature's way was best, whilst B'limbini, his cousin, was the chief exponent of the sharpened form.

It took two battalions of King Coast Rifles, half a battery of artillery and Sanders to settle the question, which became a national one.

"I wish Bosambo were to the devil before he left his country," said Sanders, irritably. "I should feel safe if that oily villain was sitting in the Ochori."

"What is the trouble?" asked Hamilton, looking up from his task—he was making cigarettes with a new machine which somebody had sent him from home.

"An infernal Bim-bi palaver," said Sanders; "the last time that happened, if I remember rightly, I had to burn crops on the right bank of the river for twenty miles to bring the Isisi to a sense of their unimportance."

"You will be able to burn crops on the left side this time," said Hamilton, cheerfully, his nimble fingers twiddling the silver rollers of his machine.

24

"I thought I had the country quiet," said Sanders, a little bitterly, "and at this moment I especially wanted it so."

"Why at this particular moment?" asked the other in surprise.

Sanders took out of the breast pocket on his uniform jacket a folded paper, and passed it across the table.

Hamilton read:

"SIR,—I have the honour to inform you that the Rt. Hon. Mr. James Blowter, his Majesty's Secretary of State for the Colonies, is expected to arrive at your station on the thirtieth inst. I trust you will give the Right Honourable gentleman every facility for studying on the spot the problems upon which he is such an authority. I have to request you to instruct all Sub-Commissioners, Inspectors, and Officers commanding troops in your division to make adequate arrangements for Mr. Blowter's comfort and protection.

"I have the honour to be, etc."

Hamilton read the letter twice.

"To study on the spot those questions upon which he is such an authority," he repeated. He was a sarcastic devil when he liked.

"The thirtieth is tomorrow," Hamilton went on, "and I suppose I am one of the officers commanding troops who must school my ribald soldiery in the art of protecting the Rt. Hon. gent."

"To be exact," said Sanders, "you are the only officer commanding troops in the territory; do what you can. You wouldn't believe it," he smiled a little shamefacedly, "I had applied for six months' leave when this came."

"Good Lord!" said Hamilton, for somehow he never associated Sanders with holidays.

What Hamilton did was very simple, because Hamilton always did things in the manner which gave him the least trouble. A word to his orderly conveyed across the parade ground, roused the sleepy bugler of the guard, and the air

25

was filled with the "Assembly." Sixty men of the Houssas paraded in anticipation of a sudden call northwards.

"My children," said Hamilton, whiffling his pliant cane, "soon there will come here a member of government who knows nothing. Also he may stray into the forest and lose himself as the bridegroom's cow strays from the field of his father-in-law, not knowing his new surroundings. Now it is to you we look for his safety—I and the government. Also Sandi, our Lord. You shall not let this stranger out of your sight, nor shall you allow approach him any such evil men as the N'gombi iron sellers or the fishing men of N'gar or makers of wooden charms, for the government has said this man must not be robbed, but must be treated well, and you of the guard shall all salute him, also, when the time arrives."

Hamilton meant no disrespect in his graphic illustration. He was dealing with a simple people who required vivid word-pictures to convince them. And certainly they found nothing undignified in the right honourable gentleman when he arrived next morning.

He was above the medium height, somewhat stout, very neat and orderly, and he twirled a waxed moustache, turning grey. He had heavy and bilious eyes, and a certain pompousness of manner distinguished him. Also an effervescent geniality which found expression in shaking hands with anybody who happened to be handy, in mechanically agreeing with all views that were put before him and immediately afterwards contradicting them; in a painful desire to be regarded as popular. In fact, in all the things which got immediately upon Sanders' nerves, this man was a sealed pattern of a bore.

He wanted to know things, but the things he wanted to know were of no importance, and the information he extracted could not be of any assistance to him. His mind was largely occupied in such vital problems as what happened to the brooms which the Houssas used to keep their quarters clean when they were worn out, and what would be the effect of an increased ration of lime juice upon the morals and discipline of the troops under Hamilton's command. Had he been less of a trial Sanders would not have allowed him to go into the interior without a stronger protest. As it was, Sanders had turned out of his own bedroom, and had put all his slender resources at the disposal of the Cabinet Minister (taking his holiday, by the way, during the long recess), and had wearied himself in order to reach some subject of interest where he and his guest could meet on common ground.

"I shall have to let him go," he said to Hamilton, when the two had met one night after Mr. Blowter had retired to bed, "I spent the whole of this afternoon discussing the comparative values of mosquito nets, and he is such a perfect ass that you cannot snub him. If he had only had the sense to bring a secretary or two he would have been easier to handle."

Hamilton laughed.

"When a man like that travels," he said, "he ought to bring somebody who knows the ways and habits of the animal. I had a bright morning with him going into the question of boots."

"But what of Mimbimi?"

"Mimbimi is rather a worry to me. I do not know him at all," said Sanders with a puzzled frown. "Ahmet, the spy, has seen one of the chiefs who attended the palaver, which apparently was very impressive. Up to now nothing has happened which would justify a movement against him; the man is possibly from the French Congo."

"Any news of Bosambo?" asked Hamilton.

Sanders shook his head.

"So far as I can learn," he said grimly, "he has gone on *Cape Coast Castle* for a real aboriginal jag. There will be trouble for Bosambo when he comes back."

"What a blessing it would be now," sighed Hamilton, "if we could turn old man Blowter into his tender keeping." And the men laughed simultaneously.

27

V

There was a time, years and years ago, when the Ochori people set a great stake on the edge of the forest by the Mountain. This they smeared with a paint made by the admixture of camwood and copal gum.

It was one of the few intelligent acts which may be credited to the Ochori in those dull days, for the stake stood for danger. It marked the boundary of the N'gombi lands beyond which it was undesirable that any man of the Ochori should go.

It was not erected without consideration. A palaver which lasted from the full of one moon to the waning of the next, sacrifices of goats and sprinkling of blood, divinations, incantations, readings of devil marks on sandy foreshores; all right and proper ceremonies were gone through before there came a night of bright moonlight when the whole Ochori nation went forth and planted that post.

Then, I believe, the people of the Ochori, having invested the post with qualities which it did not possess, went back to their homes and forgot all about it. Yet if they forgot there were nations who regarded the devil sign with some awe, and certainly Mimbimi, the newly-arisen ranger of the forest, who harried the Akasava and the Isisi, and even the N'gombi-Isisi, must have had full faith in its potency, for he never moved beyond that border. Once, so legend said, he brought his terrible warriors to the very edge of the land and paid homage to the innocent sign-post which Sanders had set up and which announced no more, in plain English, than trespassers would be prosecuted. Having done his *devoir* he retired to his forest lair. His operations were not to go without an attempted reprisal. Many parties went out against him, notably that which Tumbilimi the chief of Isisi led. He took a hundred picked men to avenge the outrage which this intruder had put upon him in daring to summon him to palaver.

Now Sugini was an arrogant man, for had he not routed the army of Bosambo? That Bosambo was not in command made no difference and did not tarnish the prestige in Tumbilimi's eyes, and though the raids upon his territory by Mimbimi had been mild, the truculent chief, disdaining the use of his full army, marched with his select column to bring in the head and feet of the man who had dared violate his territory.

Exactly what happened to Tumbilimi's party is not known; all the men who escaped from the ambush in which Mimbimi lay give a different account, and each account creditable to themselves, though the only thing which stands in their favour is that they did certainly save their lives. Certainly Tumbilimi, he of the conquering spears, came back no more, and those parts which he had threatened to detach from his enemy were in fact detached from him and were discovered one morning at the very gates of his city for his horrified subjects to marvel at. When warlike discussions arose, as they did at infrequent intervals, it was the practice of the people to send complaints to Sanders and leave him to deal with the matter. You cannot, however, lead an army against a dozen guerrilla chiefs with any profit to the army as we once discovered in a country somewhat south of Sanders' domains. Had Mimbimi's sphere of operations been confined to the river, Sanders would have laid him by the heels quickly enough, because the river brigand is easy to catch since he would starve in the forest, and if he took to the bush would certainly come back to the gleaming water for very life.

But here was a forest man obviously, who needed no river for himself, but was content to wait watchfully in the dim recesses of the woods.

Sanders sent three spies to locate him, and gave his attention to the more immediate problem of his Right Honourable guest. Mr. Joseph Blowter had decided to make a trip into the interior and the *Zaire* had been placed at his disposal. A heaven-sent riot in the bushland, sixty miles

29

west of the Residency, had relieved both Sanders and Hamilton from the necessity of accompanying the visitor, and he departed by steamer with a bodyguard of twenty armed Houssas; more than sufficient in these peaceful times.

"What about Mimbimi?" asked Hamilton under his breath as they stood on a little concrete quay, and watched the *Zaire* beating out to mid-stream.

"Mimbimi is evidently a bushman," said Sanders briefly. "He will not come to the river. Besides, he is giving the Ochori a wide berth, and it is to the Ochori that our friend is going. I cannot see how he can possibly dump himself into mischief."

Nevertheless, as a matter of precaution, Sanders telegraphed to the Administration not only the departure, but the precautions he had taken for the safety of the Minister, and the fact that neither he nor Hamilton were accompanying him on his tour of inspection "to study on the spot those problems with which he was so well acquainted."

"O.K." flashed Bob across the wires, and that was sufficient for Sanders. Of Mr. Blowter's adventures it is unnecessary to tell in detail. How he mistook every village for a city, and every city for a nation, of how he landed wherever he could and spoke long and eloquently on the blessing of civilisation, and the glories of the British flag— all this through an interpreter—of how he went into the question of basket-making and fly-fishing, and of how he demonstrated to the fishermen of the little river a method of catching fish by fly, and how he did not catch anything. All these matters might be told in great detail with no particular credit to the subject of the monograph.

In course of time he came to the Ochori land and was welcomed by Notiki, who had taken upon himself, on the strength of his rout, the position of chieftainship. This he did with one eye on the river, ready to bolt the moment Bosambo's canoe came sweeping round the bend.

Now Sanders had particularly warned Mr. Blowter that under no circumstances should he sleep ashore. He gave a variety of reasons, such as the prevalence of Beri-Beri, the insidious spread of sleeping sickness, the irritation of malaria-bearing mosquitoes, and of other insects which it would be impolite to mention in the pages of a family journal.

But Notiki had built a new hut as he said especially for his guest, and Mr. Blowter, no doubt, honoured by the attention which was shown to him, broke the restricting rule that Sanders had laid down, quitted the comfortable cabin which had been his home on the river journey, and slept in the novel surroundings of a native hut.

How long he slept cannot be told; he was awakened by a tight hand grasping his throat and a fierce voice whispering into his ear something which he rightly understood to be an admonition, a warning and a threat.

At any rate, he interpreted it as a request on the part of his captor that he should remain silent, and to this Mr. Blowter in a blue funk passively agreed. Three men caught him and bound him deftly with native rope, a gag was put into his mouth, and he was dragged cautiously through a hole which the intruders had cut in the walls of Notiki's dwelling of honour. Outside the hut door was a Houssa sentry and it must be confessed that he was not aware at the moment of Mr. Blowter's departure.

His captors spirited him by back ways to the river, dumped him into a canoe and paddled with frantic haste to the other shore.

They grounded their canoe, pulled him—inwardly quaking—to land, and hurried him to the forest. On their way they met a huntsman who had been out overnight after a leopard, and in the dark of the dawn the chief of those who had captured Mr. Blowter addressed the startled man.

"Go you to the city of Ochori," he said, "and say 'Mimbimi, the high chief who is lord of the forest of Bim-bi, sends

word that he has taken the fat white lord to his keeping, and
he shall hold him for his pleasure.'"

VI

It would appear from all the correspondence which was
subsequently published that Sanders had particularly
warned Mr. Blowter against visiting the interior, that Sir
Robert, that amiable man, had also expressed a warning,
and that the august Government itself had sent a long and
expensive telegram from Downing Street suggesting that a
trip to the Ochori country was inadvisable in the present
state of public feeling.

The hasty disposition on the part of certain journals to
blame Mr. Commissioner Sanders and his immediate
superior for the kidnapping of so important a person as a
Cabinet Minister was obviously founded upon an ignorance
of the circumstances.

Yet Sanders felt himself at fault, as a conscientious man
always will, if he has had the power to prevent a certain
happening.

Those loyal little servants of Government, carrier pigeons
—went fluttering east, south, and north, a missionary steamer
was hastily requisitioned, and Sanders embarked for the
scene of the disappearance.

Before he left he telegraphed to every likely coast town for
Bosambo.

"If that peregrinating devil had not left his country this
would not have happened," said Sanders irritably; "he
must come back and help me find the lost one."

Before any answer could come to his telegrams he had
embarked, and it is perhaps as well that he did not wait,
since none of the replies were particularly satisfactory.
Bosambo was evidently ungetatable, and the most alarming
rumour of all was that which came from Sierra Leone and

was to the effect that Bosambo had embarked for England with the expressed intention of seeking an interview with a very high personage indeed.

Now it is the fact that had Sanders died in the execution of his duty, died either from fever or as the result of scientific torturing at the hands of Akasava braves, less than a couple of lines in the London Press would have paid tribute to the work he had done or the terrible manner of his passing.

But a Cabinet Minister, captured by a cannibal tribe, offers in addition to alliterative possibilities in the headline department, a certain novelty particularly appealing to the English reader who loves above all things to have a shock or two with his breakfast bacon. England was shocked to its depths by the unusual accident which had occurred to the Right Honourable gentleman, partly because it is unusual for Cabinet Ministers to find themselves in a cannibal's hands, and partly because Mr. Blowter himself occupied a very large place in the eye of the public at home. For the first time in its history the eyes of the world were concentrated on Sanders' territory, and the Press of the world devoted important columns to dealing not only with the personality of the man who had been stolen, because they knew him well, but more or less inaccurately with the man who was charged with his recovery.

They also spoke of Bosambo "now on his way to England," and it is a fact that a small fleet of motor-boats containing Pressmen awaited the incoming coast mail at Plymouth only to discover that their man was not on board.

Happily, Sanders was in total ignorance of the stir which the disappearance created. He knew, of course, that there would be talk about it, and had gloomy visions of long reports to be written. He would have felt happier in his mind if he could have identified Mimbimi with any of the wandering chiefs he had met or had known from time to time. Mimbimi was literally a devil he did not know.

Nor could any of the cities or villages which had received a visitation give the Commissioner more definite data than he possessed. Some there were who said that Mimbimi was a tall man, very thin, knobbly at the knees, and was wounded in the foot, so that he limped. Others that he was short and very ugly, with a large head and small eyes, and that when he spoke it was in a voice of thunder.

Sanders wasted no time in useless inquiries. He threw a cloud of spies and trackers into the forest of Bim-bi and began a scientific search; snatching a few hours' sleep whenever the opportunity offered. But though the wings of his beaters touched the border line of the Ochori on the right and the Isisi on the left, and though he passed through places which hitherto had been regarded as impenetrable on account of divers devils, yet he found no trace of the cunning kidnapper, who, if the truth be told, had broken through the lines in the night, dragging an unwilling and exasperated member of the British Government at the end of a rope fastened about his person.

Then messages began to reach Sanders, long telegrams sent up from headquarters by swift canoe or rewritten on paper as fine as cigarette paper and sent in sections attached to the legs of pigeons.

They were irritating, hectoring, worrying, frantic messages. Not only from the Government, but from the kidnapped man's friends and relatives; for it seemed that this man had accumulated, in addition to a great deal of unnecessary information, quite a large and respectable family circle. Hamilton came up with a reinforcement of Houssas without achieving any notable result.

"He has disappeared as if the ground had opened and swallowed him," said Sanders bitterly. "O! Mimbimi, if I could have you now," he said with passionate intensity.

"I am sure you would be very rude to him," said Hamilton

34

soothingly. "He must be somewhere, my dear chap; do you think he has killed the poor old bird?"

Sanders shook his head.

"The lord knows what he has done or what has happened to him," he said.

It was at that moment that the messenger came. The *Zaire* was tied to the bank of the Upper Isisi on the edge of the forest of Bim-bi, and the Houssas were bivouacked on the bank, their red fires gleaming in the gathering darkness.

The messenger came from the forest boldly; he showed no fear of Houssas, but walked through their lines, waving his long stick as a bandmaster will flourish his staff. And when the sentry on the plank that led to the boat had recovered from the shock of seeing the unexpected apparition, the man was seized and led before the Commissioner.

"O, man," said Sanders, "who are you and where do you come from? Tell me what news you bring."

"Lord," said the man glibly, "I am Mimbimi's own headman."

Sanders jumped up from his chair.

"Mimbimi!" he said quickly; "tell me what message you bring from that thief!"

"Lord," said the man, "he is no thief, but a high prince."

Sanders was peering at him searchingly.

"It seems to me," he said, "that you are of the Ochori."

"Lord, I was of the Ochori," said the messenger, "but now I am with Mimbimi—his headman, following him through all manners of danger. Therefore I have no people or nation—wa! Lord, here is my message."

Sanders nodded.

"Go on," he said, "messenger of Mimbimi, and let your news be good for me."

"Master," said the man, "I come from the great one of the forest who holds all lives in his two hands, and fears not anything that lives or moves, neither devil nor Bim-bi nor

35

the ghosts that walk by night nor the high dragons in the trees——"

"Get to your message, my man," said Sanders, unpleasantly; "for I have a whip which bites sharper than the dragons in the trees and moves more swiftly that m'shamba."

The man nodded.

"Thus says Mimbimi," he resumed. "Go you to the place near the Crocodile River where Sandi sits, say Mimbimi the chief loves him, and because of his love Mimbimi will do a great thing. Also he said," the man went on, "and this is the greatest message of all. Before I speak further you must make a book of my words."

Sanders frowned. It was an unusual request from a native, for his offer to be set down in writing. "You might take a note of this, Hamilton," he said aside, "though why the deuce he wants a note of this made I cannot for the life of me imagine. Go on, messenger," he said more mildly; "for as you see my lord Hamilton makes a book."

"Thus says my lord Mimbimi," resumed the man, "that because of his love for Sandi he would give you the fat white lord whom he has taken, asking for no rods or salt in repayment, but doing this because of his love for Sandi and also because he is a just and noble man; therefore do I deliver the fat one into your hands."

Sanders gasped.

"Do you speak the truth?" he asked incredulously.

The man nodded his head.

"Where is the fat Lord?" asked Sanders. This was no time for ceremony or for polite euphemistic descriptions even of Cabinet Ministers.

"Master, he in is the forest, less than the length of the village from here, I have tied him to a tree."

Sanders raced across the plank and through the Houssa lines, dragging the messenger by the arm, and Hamilton, with a hastily summoned guard, followed. They found

Joseph Blowter tied scientifically to a gum-tree, a wedge of wood in his mouth to prevent him speaking, and he was a terribly unhappy man. Hastily the bonds were loosed, and the gag removed, and the groaning Cabinet Minister led, half carried to the *Zaire*.

He recovered sufficiently to take dinner that night, was full of his adventures, inclined perhaps to exaggerate his peril, pardonably exasperated against the man who had led him through so many dangers, real and imaginary. But, above all things, he was grateful to Sanders.

He acknowledged that he had got into his trouble through no fault of the Commissioner.

"I cannot tell you how sorry I am all this has occurred," said Sanders.

It was after dinner, and Mr. Blowter in a spotless white suit—shaved, looking a little more healthy from his enforced exercise, and certainly considerably thinner, was in the mood to take an amused view of his experience.

"One thing I have learnt, Mr. Sanders," he said, "and that is the extraordinary respect in which you are held in this country. I never spoke of you to this infernal rascal but that he bowed low, and all his followers with him; why, they almost worship you!"

If Mr. Blowter had been surprised by this experience no less surprised was Sanders to learn of it.

"This is news to me," he said dryly.

"That is your modesty, my friend," said the Cabinet Minister with a benign smile. "I, at any rate, appreciate the fact that but for your popularity I should have had short shrift from this murderous blackguard."

He went down stream the next morning, the *Zaire* over-crowded with Houssas.

"I should have liked to have left a party in the forest," said Sanders; "I shall not rest until we get this thief Mimbimi by the ear."

"I should not bother," said Hamilton dryly; "the sobering influence of your name seems to be almost as potent as my Houssas."

"Please do not be sarcastic," said Sanders sharply, he was unduly sensitive on the question of such matters as these. Nevertheless, he was happy at the end of the adventure, though somewhat embarrassed by the telegrams of congratulation which were poured upon him not only from the Administrator but from England.

"If I had done anything to deserve it I would not mind," he said.

"That is the beauty of reward," smiled Hamilton; "if you deserve things you do not get them, if you do not deserve them they come in cartloads, you have to take the thick with the thin. Think of the telegrams which ought to have come and did not."

They took farewell of Mr. Blowter on the beach, the surf-boat waiting to carry him to a mail steamer decorated for the occasion with strings of flags.

"There is one question which I would like to ask you," said Sanders, "and it is one which for some reason I have forgotten to ask before—can you describe Mimbimi to me so that I may locate him? He is quite unknown to us."

Mr. Blowter frowned thoughtfully.

"He is difficult to describe! all natives are alike to me," he said slowly. "He is rather tall, well-made, good-looking for a native, and talkative."

"Talkative!" said Sanders quickly.

"In a way; he can speak a little English," said the Cabinet Minister, "and evidently has some sort of religious training, because he spoke of Mark and Luke, and the various Apostles as one who had studied possibly at a missionary school."

"Mark and Luke," almost whispered Sanders, a great light dawning upon him. "Thank you very much. I think you said he always bowed when my name was mentioned?"

"Invariably!" smiled the Cabinet Minister.

"Thank you, sir." Sanders shook hands.

"Oh, by the way, Mr. Sanders," said Blowter, turning back from the boat, "I suppose you know that you have been gazetted C.M.G.?"

Sanders flushed red and stammered: "C.M.G."

"It is an indifferent honour for one who has rendered such service to the country as you," said the complacent Mr. Blowter profoundly; "but the Government feel that it is the least they can do for you after your unusual effort on my behalf and they have asked me to say to you that they will not be unmindful of your future."

He left Sanders standing as though frozen to the spot.

Hamilton was the first to congratulate him.

"My dear chap, if ever a man deserved the C.M.G. it is you," he said.

It would be absurd to say that Sanders was not pleased. He was certainly not pleased at the method by which it came, but he should have known, being acquainted with the ways of Governments, that this was the reward of cumulative merit. He walked back in silence to the Residency, Hamilton keeping pace by his side.

"By the way, Sanders," he said, "I have just had a pigeon-post from the river—Bosambo is back in the Ochori country. Have you any idea how he arrived there?"

"I think I have," said Sanders, with a grim little smile, "and I think I shall be calling on Bosambo very soon."

But that was a threat he was never destined to put into execution. That same evening came a wire from Bob.

"Your leave is granted: Hamilton is to act as Commissioner in your temporary absence. I am sending Lieutenant Francis Augustus Tibbets to take charge of Houssas."

"And who the devil is Francis Augustus Tibbetts?" said Sanders and Hamilton with one voice.

CHAPTER I

HAMILTON OF THE HOUSSAS

SANDERS turned to the rail and cast a wistful glance at the low-lying shore. He saw one corner of the white Residency, showing through the sparse *isisi* palm at the end of the big garden—a smudge of green on yellow from this distance.

"I hate going—even for six months," he said.

Hamilton of the Houssas, with laughter in his blue eyes, and his fumed-oak face—lean and wholesome it was—all a-twitch, whistled with difficulty.

"Oh, yes, I shall come back again," said Sanders, answering the question in the tune. "I hope things will go well in my absence."

"How can they go well?" asked Hamilton, gently. "How can the Isisi live, or the Akasava sow his barbarous potatoes, or the sun shine, or the river run when Sandi Sitani is no longer in the land?"

"I wouldn't have worried," Sanders went on, ignoring the insult, "if they'd put a good man in charge; but to give a pudden-headed soldier——"

"We thank you!" bowed Hamilton.

"—— with little or no experience——"

"An insolent lie—and scarcely removed from an unqualified lie!" murmured Hamilton.

"To put him in my place!" apostrophised Sanders, tilting back his helmet the better to appeal to the heavens.

"'Orrible! 'Orrible!" said Hamilton; "and now I seem to catch the accusing eye of the chief officer, which means that he wants me to hop. God bless you, old man!"

His sinewy paw caught the other's in a grip that left both hands numb at the finish.

40

"Keep well," said Sanders in a low voice, his hand on Hamilton's back, as they walked to the gangway. "Watch the Isisi and sit on Bosambo—especially Bosambo, for he is a mighty slippery devil."

"Leave me to deal with Bosambo," said Hamilton firmly, as he skipped down the companion to the big boat that rolled and tumbled under the coarse skin of the ship.

"I *am* leaving you," said Sanders with a chuckle.

He watched the Houssa pick a finicking way to the stern of the boat; saw the solemn faces of his rowmen as they bent their naked backs, gripping their clumsy oars. And to think that they and Hamilton were going back to the familiar life, to the dear full days he knew! Sanders coughed and swore at himself.

"Oh, Sandi!" called the headman of the boat, as she went lumbering over the clear green swell, "remember us, your servants!"

"I will remember, man," said Sanders, a-choke, and turned quickly to his cabin.

Hamilton sat in the stern of the surf-boat, humming a song to himself; but he felt awfully solemn, though in his pocket reposed a commission sealed redly and largely on parchment and addressed to: "Our well-beloved Patrick George Hamilton, Lieutenant, of our 133rd 1st Royal Hertford Regiment. Seconded for service in our 9th Regiment of Houssas—Greeting . . ."

"Master," said his Kroo servant, who waited his landing, "you lib for dem big house?"

"I lib," said Hamilton.

"Dem big house," was the Residency, in which a temporarily appointed Commissioner must take up his habitation, if he is to preserve the dignity of his office.

"Let us pray!" said Hamilton earnestly, addressing himself to a small snapshot photograph of Sanders, which stood on a side table. "Let us pray that the barbarian of his kindness will sit quietly till you return, my Sanders—for the Lord knows what trouble I'm going to get into before you return!"

The incoming mail brought Francis Augustus Tibbetts, Lieutenant of the Houssas, raw to the land, but as cheerful as the devil—a straight stick of a youth, with hair brushed back from his forehead, a sun-peeled nose, a wonderful collection of baggage, and all the gossip of London.

"I'm afraid you'll find I'm rather an ass, sir," he said, saluting stiffly. "I've only just arrived on the Coast an' I'm simply bubbling over with energy, but I'm rather short in the brain department."

Hamilton, glaring at his subordinate through his monocle, grinned sympathetically.

"I'm not a whale of erudition myself," he confessed. "What is your name, sir?"

"Francis Augustus Tibbetts, sir."

"I shall call you Bones," said Hamilton decisively.

Lieut. Tibbetts saluted. "They called me Conk at Sandhurst, sir," he suggested.

"Bones!" said Hamilton, definitely.

"Bones it is, skipper," said Mr. Tibbetts; "an' now all this beastly formality is over we'll have a bottle to celebrate things." And a bottle they had.

It was a splendid evening they spent, dining on chicken and palm-oil chop, rice pudding and sweet potatoes. Hamilton sang, "Who wouldn't be a soldier in the Army?" and—by request—in his shaky falsetto baritone, "My heart is in the Highlands"; and Lieut. Tibbetts gave a lifelike imitation of Frank Tinney, which convulsed, not alone his superior officer, but some two-and-forty men of the Houssas who were unauthorised spectators through various windows and door cracks and ventilating gauzes.

Bones was the son of a man who had occupied a position of some importance on the Coast, and though the young man's upbringing had been in England, he had the inestimable advantage of a very thorough grounding in the native dialect, not only from Tibbetts, senior, but from the two native servants with whom the boy had grown up.

"I suppose there is a telegraph line to headquarters?" asked Bones that night before they parted.

"Certainly, my dear lad," replied Hamilton. "We had it laid down when we heard you were coming."

"Don't flither!" pleaded Bones, giggling convulsively; "but the fact is I've got a couple of dozen tickets in the Cambridgeshire Sweepstake, an' a dear pal of mine—chap named Goldfinder, a rare and delicate bird—has sworn to wire me if I've drawn a horse. D'ye think I'll draw a horse?"

"I shouldn't think you could draw a cow," said Hamilton. "Go to bed."

"Look here, Ham——" began Lieut. Bones.

"To bed! you insubordinate devil!" said Hamilton, sternly.

In the meantime there was trouble in the Akasava country.

II

Scarcely had Sanders left the land, when the *lokali* of the Lower Isisi sent the news thundering in waves of sound.

Up and down the river and from village to village, from town to town, across rivers, penetrating dimly to the quiet deeps of the forest the story was flung. N'gori, the Chief of the Akasava, having some grievance against the Government over a question of fine for failure to collect according to law, waited for no more than this intelligence of Sandi's going. His swift loud drums called his people to a dance-of-many-days. A dance-of-many-days spells "spears" and spears spell trouble. Bosambo heard the message in the still of the early night, gathered five hundred fighting men,

43

swept down on the Akasava city in the drunken dawn, and carried away two thousand spears of the sodden N'gori.

A sobered Akasava city woke up and rubbed its eyes to find strange Ochori sentinels in the street and Bosambo in a sky-blue table-cloth, edged with golden fringe, stalking majestically through the high places of the city.

"This I do," said Bosambo to a shocked N'gori, "because my lord Sandi placed me here to hold the king's peace."

"Lord Bosambo," said the king sullenly, "what peace do I break when I summon my young men and maidens to dance?"

"Your young men are thieves, and it is written that the maidens of the Akasava are married once in ten thousand moons," said Bosambo calmly; "and also, N'gori, you speak to a wise man who knows that clockety-clock-clock on a drum spells war."

There was a long and embarrassing silence.

"Now, Bosambo," said N'gori, after a while, "you have my spears and your young men hold the streets and the river. What will you do? Do you sit here till Sandi returns and there is law in the land?"

This was the one question which Bosambo had neither the desire nor the ability to answer. He might swoop down upon a warlike people, surprising them to their abashment, rendering their armed forces impotent, but exactly what would happen afterwards he had not foreseen.

"I go back to my city," he said.

"And my spears?"

"Also they go with me," said Bosambo.

They eyed each other: Bosambo straight and muscular, a perfect figure of a man, N'gori grizzled and skinny, his brow furrowed with age.

"Lord," said N'gori mildly, "if you take my spears you leave me bound to my enemies. How may I protect my villages against oppression by evil men of Isisi?"

44

Bosamba sniffed—a sure sign of mental perturbation. All that N'gori said was true. Yet if he left the spears there would be trouble for him. Then a bright thought flicked:

"If bad men come you shall send for me and I will bring my fine young soldiers. The palaver is finished."

With this course N'gori must feign agreement. He watched the departing army—paddlers sitting on swathes of filched spears. Once Bosambo was out of sight, N'gori collected all the convertible property of his city and sent it in ten canoes to the edge of the N'gombi country, for N'gombi folk are wonderful makers of spears and have a saleable stock hidden against emergency.

For the space of a month there was enacted a comedy of which Hamilton was ignorant. Three days after Bosambo had returned in triumph to his city, there came a frantic call for succour—a rolling, terrified rat-a-plan of sound which the *lokai* man of the Ochori village read.

"Lord," said he, waking Bosambo in the dead of night, "there has come down a signal from the Akasava, who are pressed by their enemies and have no spears."

Bosambo was in the dark street instanter, his booming war-drum calling urgently. Twenty canoes filled with fighting men, paddling desperately with the stream, raced to the aid of the defenceless Akasava.

At dawn, on the beach of the city, N'gori met his ally. "I thank all my little gods you have come, my lord," said he, humbly; "for in the night one of my young men saw an Isisi army coming against us."

"Where is the army?" demanded a weary Bosambo.

"Lord, it has not come," said N'gori, glibly; "for hearing of your lordship and your swift canoes, I think it had run away."

Bosambo's force paddled back to the Ochori city the next day. Two nights after, the call was repeated—this time with greater detail. An N'gombi force of countless spears had seized the village of Doozani and was threatening the capital.

Again Bosambo carried his spears to a killing, and again was met by an apologetic N'gori.

"Lord, it was a lie which a sick maiden spread," he explained, "and my stomach is filled with sorrow that I should have brought the mighty Bosambo from his wife's bed on such a night." For the dark hours had been filled with rain and tempest, and Bosambo had nearly lost one canoe by wreck.

"Oh, fool!" said he, justly exasperated, "have I nothing to do—I, who have all Sandi's high and splendid business in hand—but I must come through the rain because a sick maiden sees visions?"

"Bosambo, I am a fool," agreed N'gori, meekly, and again his rescuer returned home.

"Now," said N'gori, "we will summon a secret palaver, sending messengers for all men to assemble at the rise of the first moon. For the N'gombi have sent me new spears, and when next the dog Bosambo comes, weary with rowing, we will fall upon him and there will be no more Bosambo left; for Sandi is gone and there is no law in the land."

III

Curiously enough, at that precise moment, the question of law was a very pressing one with two young Houssa officers who sat on either side of Sanders' big table, wet towels about their heads, mastering the intricacies of the military code; for Tibbetts was entering for an examination and Hamilton, who had only passed his own by a fluke, had rashly offered to coach him.

"I hope you understand this, Bones," said Hamilton, staring up at his subordinate and running his finger along the closely printed pages of the book before him.

46

"'Any person subject to military law,'" read Hamilton impressively, "'who strikes or ill-uses his superior officer shall, if an officer, suffer death or such less punishment as in this Act mentioned.' Which means," said Hamilton, wisely, "that if you and I are in action and you call me a liar, and I give you a whack on the jaw——"

"You get shot," said Bones, admiringly, "an' a rippin' good idea, too!"

"If, on the other hand," Hamilton went on, "I called you a liar—which I should be justified in doing—and you give me a whack on the jaw, I'd make you sorry you were ever born."

"That's military law, is it?" asked Bones, curiously.

"It is," said Hamilton.

"Then let's chuck it," said Bones, and shut up his book with a bang. "I don't want any book to teach me what to do with a feller that calls me a liar. I'll go you one game of picquet, for nuts."

"You're on," said Hamilton.

      *   *   *   *   *

"My nuts I think, sir."

Bones carefully counted the heap which his superior had pushed over, "And—hullo! what the dooce do you want?"

Hamilton followed the direction of the other's eyes. A man stood in the doorway, naked but for the wisp of skirt at his waist. Hamilton got up quickly, for he recognised the chief of Sandi's spies.

"O Kelili," said Hamilton, in his easy Bomongo tongue, "why do you come and from whence?"

"From the island over against the Ochori, Lord," croaked the man, dry-throated. "Two pigeons I sent, but these the hawks took—a fisherman saw one taken by the Kasai, and my own brother, who lives in the Village of Irons, saw the other go—though he flew swiftly."

47

Hamilton's grave face set rigidly, for he smelt trouble. You do not send pleasant news by pigeons.

"Speak," he said.

"Lord," said Kelili, "there is to be a killing palaver between the Ochori and the Akasava on the first rise of the full moon, for N'gori speaks of Bosambo evilly, and says that the Chief has raided him. In what manner these things will come about," Kelili went on, with the lofty indifference of one who had done his part of the business, so that he had left no room for carelessness, "I do not know, but I have warned all eyes of the Government to watch."

Bones followed the conversation without difficulty.

"What do people say?" asked Hamilton.

"Lord, they say that Sandi has gone and there is no law."

Hamilton of the Houssas grinned. "Oh, ain't there?" said he, in English, vilely.

"Ain't there?" repeated an indignant Bones, "we'll jolly well show old Thingummy what's what."

Bosambo received an envoy from the Chief of the Akasava, and the envoy brought with him presents of dubious value and a message to the effect that N'gori spent much of his waking moments in wondering how he might best serve his brother Bosambo. "The right arm in which I and my people lean and the bright eyes through which I see beauty."

Bosambo returned the messenger, with presents more valueless, and an assurance of friendship more sonorous, more complete in rhetoric and aptness of hyperbole, and when the messenger had gone Bosambo showed his appreciation of N'gori's love by doubling the guard about the Ochori city and sending a strong picket under his chief headman to hold the river bend.

"Because," said this admirable philosopher, "life is like certain roots: some that taste sweet and are bitter in the end, and some that are vile to the lips and pleasant to the stomach."

48

It was a wild night, being in the month of rains. M'shimba M'shamba was abroad, walking with his devastating feet through the forest, plucking up great trees by their roots and tossing them aside as though they were so many canes. There was a roaring of winds and a crashing of thunders, and the blue-white lightning snicked in and out of the forest or tore sprawling cracks in the sky. In the Ochori city they heard the storm grumbling across the river and were awakened by the incessant lightning—so incessant that the weaver birds who lived in palms that fringed the Ochori streets came chattering to life.

It was too loud a noise, that M'shimba M'shamba made for the *lokali* man of the Ochori to hear the message that N'gori sent—the panic-message designed to lure Bosambo to the newly-purchased spears.

Bones heard it—Bones, standing on the bridge of the *Zaire* pounding away upstream, steaming past the Akasava city in a sheet of rain.

"Wonder what the jolly old row is?" he muttered to himself, and summoned his sergeant. "Ali," said he, in faultless Arabic, "what beating of drums are these?"

"Lord," said the sergeant, uneasily, "I do not know, unless they be to warn us not to travel at night. I am your man, Master," said he in a fret, "yet never have I travelled with so great a fear: even our Lord Sandi does not move by night, though the river is his own child."

"It is written," said Bones, cheerfully, and as the sergeant saluted, and turned away, the reckless Houssa made a face at the darkness. "If old man Ham would give me a month or two on the river," he mused, "I'd set 'em alight, by Jove!"

By the miraculous interposition of Providence Bones reached the Ochori village in the grey clouded dawn, and Bosambo, early astir, met the lank figure of the youth, his slick sword dangling, his long revolver holster strapped to his side, and his helmet on the back of his head, an eager warrior looking for trouble.

"Lord, of you I have heard," said Bosambo, politely; "here in the Ochori country we talk of no other thing than the new, thin Lord whose beautiful nose is like the red flowers of the forest."

"Leave my nose alone," said Bones, unpleasantly, "and tell me, Chief, what killing palaver in this I hear? I come from Government to right all wrongs—this is evidently his nibs, Bosambo." The last passage was in his own native tongue and Bosambo beamed.

"Yes, sah!" said he in the English of the Coast. "I be Bosambo, good chap, fine chap; you, sah, you look um— you see um—Bosambo!"

He slapped his chest, and Bones unbent.

"Look here, old sport," he said affably: "what the dooce is all this shindy about—hey?"

"No shindy, sah!" said Bosambo—being sure that all people of his city were standing about at a respectful distance, awe-stricken by the sight of their chief on equal terms with this new white lord.

"Dem feller he lib for Akasava, sah—he be bad feller: I be good feller, sah—C'istian, sah! Matt'ew, Marki, Luki, Johni—I savvy dem fine."

Happily, Bones continued the conversation in the tongue of the land. Then he learned of the dance which Bosambo had frustrated, of the spears taken, and these he saw stacked in three huts.

Bones, despite the character he gave himself, was no fool, and, moreover, he had the advantage of knowing of the new N'gombi spears that were going out to the Akasava day by day; and when Bosambo told of the midnight summons that had come to him, Bones did the rapid exercise of mental figuring which is known as putting two and two together.

He wagged his head when Bosambo had finished his

recital, did this general of twenty-one. "You're a jolly old sportsman, Bosambo," he said, very seriously, "and you're in the dooce of a hole, if you only knew it. But you trust old Bones—he'll see you through. By Gad!"

Bosambo, bewildered but resourceful, hearing, without understanding, replied: "I be fine feller, sah!"

"You bet your life you are, old funnyface," agreed Bones, and screwed his eyeglass in the better to survey his protégé.

IV

Chief N'gori organised a surprise party for Bosambo, and took so much trouble with the details, that, because of his sheer thoroughness, he deserved to have succeeded. *Lokali* men concealed in the bush were waiting to announce the coming of the rescue party, when N'gori sent his cry for help crashing across the world. Six hundred spearmen stood ready to embark in fifty canoes, and five hundred more waited on either bank ready to settle with any survivors of the Ochori who found their way to land.

The best of plans are subject to the banal reservation, "weather permitting," and the signal intended to bring Bosambo to his destruction was swallowed up in the bellow-ings of the storm.

"This night being fine," said N'gori, showing his teeth, "Bosambo will surely come."

His Chief Counsellor, an ancient man of the royal tribe,[1] had unexpected warnings to offer. A man had seen a man, who had caught a glimpse of the *Zaire* butting her way up-stream in the dead of night. Was it wise, when the devil Sandi waited to smite, and so close at hand, to engage in so high an adventure?

"Old man, there is a hut in the forest for you," said N'gori,

[1] That which I call the Akasava proper is the very small, dominant clan of a tribe which is loosely called "Akasava," but is really Bowongo.

with significance, and the Counsellor wilted, because the huts in the forest are for the sick, the old, and the mad, and here they are left to starve and die; "for," N'gori went on, "All men know that Sandi has gone to his people across the black waters, and the M'ilitani rules. Also, in nights of storms there are men who see even devils."

With more than ordinary care he prepared for the final settling with Bosambo the Robber, and there is a suggestion that he was encouraged by the chiefs of other lands, who had grown jealous of the Ochori and their offensive rectitude. Be that as it may, all things were made ready, even to the knives of sacrifice and the young saplings which had not been employed by the Akasava for their grisly work since the Year of Hangings.

At an hour before midnight the tireless *lokali* sent out its call:

"We of the Akasava"	(four long rolls and a quick succession of taps)
"Danger threatens"	(a long roll, a short roll, and a triple tap-tap)
"Isisi fighting"	(rolls punctuated by shorter tattoos)
"Come to me"	(a long crescendo roll and patter of taps)
"Ochori"	(nine rolls, curiously like the yelping of a dog)

So the message went out: every village heard and repeated. The Isisi threw the call northward; the N'gombi village sent it westward, and presently first the Isisi, then the N'gombi, heard the faint answer: "Coming—the Breaker of Lives." and returned the message to N'gori.

"Now I shall also break lives," said N'gori, and sacrificed a goat to his success.

Sixteen hundred fighting men waited for the signal from the hidden *lokali* player, on the far side of the river bend. At the first hollow rattle of his sticks, N'gori pushed off in his royal canoe.

"Kill!" he roared, and went out in the white light of dawn to greet ten Ochori canoes, riding in fanshape formation, having as their centre a white and speckless *Zaire* alive with Houssas and overburdened with the slim muzzles of Hotchkiss guns.

"Oh, Ko!" said N'gori dismally, "this is a bad palaver!"

In the centre of his city, before a reproving squad of Houssas, a dumb man, taken in the act of armed aggression, N'gori stood.

"You're a naughty boy," said Bones, reproachfully, "and if jolly old Sanders were here—my word, you'd catch it!"

N'gori listened to the unknown tongue, worried by its mystery. "Lord, what happens to me!" he asked.

Bones looked very profound and scratched his head. He looked at the Chief, at Bosambo, at the river all aglow in the early morning sunlight, at the *Zaire*, with her sinister guns aglitter, and then back at the Chief. He was not well versed in the dialect of the Akasava, and Bosambo must be his interpreter.

"Very serious offence, old friend," said Bones, solemnly; "awfully serious—muckin' about with spears and all that sort of thing. I'll have to make a dooce of an example of you—yes, by Heaven!"

Bosambo heard and imperfectly understood. He looked about for a likely tree where an unruly chief might sway with advantage to the community.

"You're a bad, bad boy," said Bones, shaking his head; "tell him."

"Yes, sah!" said Bosambo.

"Tell him he's fined ten dollars."

But Bosambo did not speak; there are moments too full for words and this was one of them.

CHAPTER II

THE DISCIPLINARIANS

LIEUTENANT AUGUSTUS TIBBETTS of the Houssas stood at attention before his chief. He stood as straight as a ramrod, his hands to his sides, his eyeglass jammed in his eye, and Hamilton of the Houssas looked at him sorrowfully.

"Bones, you're an ass!" he said at last.

"Yes, sir," said Bones.

"I sent you to Ochori to prevent a massacre, you catch a chief in the act of ambushing an enemy and instead of chucking him straight into the Village of Irons you fine him ten dollars."

"Yes, sir," said Bones.

There was a painful silence.

"Well, you're an ass!" said Hamilton, who could think of nothing better to say.

"Yes, sir," said Bones; "I think you're repeating yourself, sir. I seem to have heard a similar observation before."

"You've made Bosambo and the whole of the Ochori as sick as monkeys, and you've made me look a fool."

"Hardly my responsibility, sir," said Bones, gently.

"I hardly know what to do with you," said Hamilton, drawing his pipe from his pocket and slowly charging it. "Naturally, Bones, I can never let you loose again on the country." He lit his pipe and puffed thoughtfully. "And of course——"

"Pardon me, sir," said Bones, still uncomfortably erect, "this is intended to be a sort of official inquiry an' all that sort of thing, isn't it?"

"It is," said Hamilton.

"Well, sir," said Bones, "may I ask you not to smoke?

54

When a chap's honour an' reputation an' all that sort of thing is being weighed in the balance, sir, believe me, smokin' isn't decent—it isn't really, sir."

Hamilton looked round for something to throw at his critic and found a tolerably heavy book, but Bones dodged and fielded it dexterously. "And if you must chuck things at me, sir," he added, as he examined the title on the back of the missile, "will you avoid as far as possible usin' the sacred volumes of the Army List? It hurts me to tell you this, sir, but I've been well brought up."

"What's the time?" asked Hamilton, and his second-in-command examined his watch.

"Ten to tiffin," he said. "Good Lord, we've been gassin' an hour. Any news from Sanders?"

"He's in town—that's all I know—but don't change the serious subject, Bones. Everybody is awfully disgusted with you—Sanders would have at least brought him to trial."

"I couldn't do it, sir," said Bones, firmly. "Poor old bird! He looked such an ass, an', moreover, reminded me so powerfully of an aunt of mine that I simply couldn't do it."

No doubt but that Lieut. Francis Augustus Tibbets of the Houssas, with his sun-burnt nose, his large saucer eyes, and his air of solemn innocence, had shaken the faith of the impressionable folk. This much Hamilton was to learn: for Tibbetts had been sent with a party of Houssas to squash effectively an incipient rebellion in the Akasava, and having caught N'gori in the very act of most treacherously and most damnably preparing an ambush for a virtuous Bosambo, Chief of the Ochori, had done no more than fine him ten dollars.

And this was in a land where even the Spanish dollar had never been seen save by Bosambo, who was reported to have more than his share of silver in a deep hole beneath the floor of his hut.

Small wonder that Captain Hamilton held an informal

55

court-martial of one, the closing stages of which I have described, and sentenced his wholly inefficient subordinate to seven days' field exercise in the forest with half a company of Houssas.

"Oh, dash it, you don't mean that?" asked Bones in dismay when the finding of the court was conveyed to him at lunch.

"I do," said Hamilton firmly. "I'd be failing in my job of work if I didn't make you realise what a perfect ass you are."

"Perfect—yes," protested Bones, "ass—no. Fact is, dear old fellow, I've a temperament. You aren't going to make me go about in that beastly forest diggin' rifle pits an' pitchin' tents an' all that sort of dam' nonsense; it's too grisly to think about."

"None the less," said Hamilton, "you will do it whilst I go north to sit on the heads of all who endeavour to profit by your misguided leniency. I shall be back in time for the Administration Inspection—don't for the love of heaven forget that His Excellency——"

"Bless his jolly old heart!" murmured Bones.

"That His Excellency is paying his annual visit on the twenty-first."

A ray of hope shot through the gloom of Lieut. Tibbets' mind.

"Under the circumstances, dear old friend, don't you think it would be best to chuck that silly idea of field training? What about sticking up a board and gettin' the chaps to paint, 'Welcome to the United Territories,' or 'God bless our Home,' or something."

Hamilton withered him with a glance.

His last words, shouted from the bridge of the *Zaire* as her stern wheel went threshing ahead, were, "Remember, Bones! No shirking!"

"*Honi soit qui mal y pense!*" roared Bones.

Hamilton had evidence enough of the effect which the leniency of his subordinate had produced. News travels fast, and the Akasava are great talkers. Hamilton, coming to the Isisi city on his way up the river, found a crowd on the beach to watch his mooring, their arms folded hugging their sides—sure gesture of indifferent idleness—but neither the paramount chief, nor his son, nor any of his counsellors awaited the steamer to pay their respects.

Hamilton sent for them and still they did not come, sending a message that they were sick. So Hamilton went striding through the street of the city, his long sword flapping at his side, four Houssas padding swiftly in his rear at their curious jog-trot. B'sano, the young chief of the Isisi, came out lazily from his hut and stood with outstretched feet and arms akimbo watching the nearing Houssa, and he had no fear, for it was said that now Sandi was away from the country no man had the authority to punish.

And the counsellors behind B'sano had their bunched spears and their wicker-work shields, contrary to all custom —as Sanders had framed the custom.

"O chief," said Hamilton, with that ready smile of his, "I waited for you and you did not come."

"Soldier," said B'sano, insolently, "I am the king of these people and answerable to none save my lord Sandi, who, as you know, is gone from us."

"That I know," said the patient Houssa, "and because it is in my heart to show all people what manner of law Sandi has left behind, I fine you and your city ten thousand *matakos* that you shall remember that the law lives, though Sandi is in the moon, though all rulers change and die."

A slow gleam of contempt came to the chief's eyes.

"Soldier," said he, "I do not pay *matako—wa!*"

He stumbled back, his mouth agape with fear. The long

57

barrel of Hamilton's revolver rested coldly on his bare stomach.

"We will have a fire," said Hamilton, and spoke to his sergeant in Arabic. "Here in the centre of the city we will make a fire of proud shields and unlawful spears."

One by one the counsellors dropped their wicker shields upon the fire which the Houssa sergeant had kindled, and as they dropped them, the sergeant scientifically handcuffed the advisers of the Isisi chief in couples.

"You shall find other counsellors, B'sano," said Hamilton, as the men were led to the *Zaire*. "See that I do not come bringing with me a new chief."

"Lord," said the chief humbly, "I am your dog."

Not alone was B'sano at fault. Up and down the road old grievances awaited settlement: there were scores to adjust, misunderstandings to remove. Mostly these misunderstandings had to do with important questions of tribal superiority and might only be definitely tested by sanguinary combat.

Also picture a secret order, ruthlessly suppressed by Sanders, and practised by trembling men, each afraid of the other despite their oaths; and the fillip it received when the news went forth—"Sandi has gone—there is no law."

This was a fine time for the dreamers of dreams and for the men who saw portends and understood the wisdom of Ju-jus.

Bemebibi, chief of the Lesser Isisi, was too fat a man for a dreamer, for visions run with countable ribs and a cough. Nor was he tall nor commanding by any standard. He had broad shoulders and a short neck. His head was round, and his eyes were cunning and small. He was an irritable man, had a trick of beating his counsellors when they displeased him, and was a ready destroyer of men.

Some say that he practised sacrifice in the forests, he and the members of his society, but none spoke with any certainty or authority, for Bemebibi was chief, alike of a community and an order. In the Lesser Isisi alone, the White Ghosts had flourished in spite of every effort of the Administration to stamp them out.

It was a society into which the hazardous youth of the Isisi were initiated joyfully, for there is little difference in the temperament of youth, whether it wears a cloth about its loins or lavender spats upon its feet.

Thus it came about that one-half of the adult male population of the Lesser Isisi had sworn by the letting of blood and the rubbing of salt:

(1) To hop upon one foot for a spear's length every night and morning.
(2) To love all ghosts and speak gently of devils.
(3) To be dumb and blind and to throw spears swiftly for the love of the White Ghosts.

One night Bemebibi went into the forest with six highmen of his order. They came to a secret place at a pool, and squatted in a circle, each man laying his hands on the soles of his feet in the prescribed fashion.

"Snakes live in holes," said Bemebibi conventionally. "Ghosts dwell by water and all devils sit in the bodies of little birds."

This they repeated after him, moving their heads from side to side slowly.

"This is a good night," said the chief, when the ritual was ended, "for now I see the end of our great thoughts. Sandi is gone and M'ilitani is by the place where the three rivers meet, and he has come in fear. Also by magic I have learnt that he is terrified because he knows me to be an awful man. Now, I think, it is time for all ghosts to strike swiftly."

He spoke with emotion, swaying his body from side to side after the manner of orators. His voice grew thick and husky as the immensity of his design grew upon him.

"There is no law in the land," he sang. "Sandi has gone, and only a little, thin man punishes in fear. Militini has blood like water—let us sacrifice."

One of his highmen disappeared into the dark forest and came back soon, dragging a half-witted youth, named Ko'so, grinning and mumbling and content till the curved N'gombi knife, that his captor wielded, came "snack" to his neck and then he spoke no more.

Too late Hamilton came through the forest with his twenty Houssas. Bemebibi saw the end and was content to make a fight for it, as were his partners in crime.

"Use your bayonets," said Hamilton briefly, and flicked out his long, white sword. Bemebibi lunged at him with his stabbing spear, and Hamilton caught the poisoned spearhead on the steel guard, touched it aside, and drove forward straight and swiftly from his shoulder.

"Bury all these men," said Hamilton, and spent a beastly night in the forest.

So passed Bemebibi, and his people gave him up to the ghosts, him and his highmen.

There were other problems less tragic, to be dealt with, a Bosambo rather grieved than sulking, a haughty N'gori to be kicked to a sense of his unimportance, chiefs, major and minor, to be brought into a condition of penitence.

Hamilton went zigzagging up the river swiftly. He earned for himself in those days the name of "Dragon-fly," or its native equivalent, and the illustration was apt, for it seemed that the *Zaire* would poise, buzzing angrily, then dart off in unexpected directions, and the spirit of complacency which had settled upon the land gave place to one of apprehension, which, in the old days, followed the arrival of Sanders in a mood of reprisal.

Hamilton sent a letter by canoe to his second-in-command. It started simply:

"Bones—I will not call you 'dear Bones,'" it went on

with a hint of the rancour in the writer's heart, "for you are not dear to me. I am striving to clear up the mess you have made so that when His Excellency arrives I shall be able to show him a law-abiding country. I have missed you, Bones, but had you been near on more occasions than one, I should not have missed you. Bones, were you ever kicked as a boy? Did any good fellow ever get you by the scruff of your neck and the seat of your trousers and chuck you into an evil-smelling pond? Try to think and send me the name of the man who did this, that I may send him a letter of thanks.

"Your absurd weakness has kept me on the move for days. Oh, Bones, Bones! I am in a sweat, lest even now you are tampering with the discipline of my Houssas—lest you are handing round tea and cake to the Alis and Ahmets and Mustaphas of my soldiers; lest you are brightening their evenings with imitations of Frank Tinney and fanning the flies from their sleeping forms," the letter went on.

"Cad!" muttered Bones, as he read this bit.

There were six pages couched in this strain, and at the end six more of instruction. Bones was in the forest when the letter came to him, unshaven, weary, and full of trouble.

He hated work, he loathed field exercise, he regarded bridge-building over imaginary streams, and the whole infernal curriculum of military training, as being peculiarly within the province of the boy scouts and wholly beneath the dignity of an officer of the Houssas. And he felt horribly guilty as he read Hamilton's letter, for the night before it came he had most certainly entertained his company with a banjo rendering of the Soldier's Chorus from *Faust*.

He rumpled his beautiful hair, jammed down his helmet, squared his shoulders, and, with a fiendish expression on his face—an expression intended by Bones to represent a stern, unbending devotion to duty, he stepped forth from his tent determined to undo what mischief he had done, and earn, if not the love, at least the respect of his people.

There is in all services a subtle fear and hope. They have to do less with material consequence than with a sense of harmony which rejects the discordance of failure. Also Hamilton was a human man, who, whilst he respected Sanders and had a profound regard for his qualities, nourished a secret faith that he might so carry on the work of the heaven-born Commissioner without demanding the charity of his superiors.

He wished—not unnaturally—to spread a triumphant palm to his country and say "Behold! There are the talents that Sanders left—I have increased them, by my care, two-fold."

He came down stream in some haste, having completed the work of pacification and stopped at the Village of Irons long enough to hand to the Houssa warder four unhappy counsellors of the Isisi king.

"Keep these men for service against our lord Sandi's return."

At Bosinkusu he was delayed by a storm, a mad, whirling brute of a storm that lashed the waters of the river and swept the *Zaire* broadside on towards the shore. At M'idibi, the villagers, whose duty it was to cut and stack wood for the Government steamers, had gone into a forest to meet a celebrated witch-doctor, gambling on the fact that there was another wooding village ten miles down stream and that Hamilton would choose that for the restocking of his boat.

So that beyond a thin skeleton pile of logs on the river's edge—set up to deceive the casual observer as he passed and approved of their industry—there was no wood and Hamilton had to set his men to wood-cutting.

He had nearly completed the heart-breaking work when the villagers returned in a body, singing an unmusical song and decked about with ropes of flowers.

"Now," explained the headman, "we have been to a palaver with a holy man and he has promised us that some day there will come to us a great harvest of corn which will be reaped by magic and laid at our doors whilst we sleep."

"And I," said the exasperated Houssa, "promise you a great harvest of whips that, so far from coming in your sleep, will keep you awake."

"Master, we did not know that you would come so soon," said the humble headman; "also there was a rumour that your lordship had been drowned in the storm and your *puc-a-puc* sunk, and my young men were happy because there would be no more wood to cut."

The *Zaire*, fuel replenished, slipped down the river, Hamilton leaning over the rail promising unpleasant happenings as the boat drifted out from the faithless village. He had cut things very fine, and could do no more than hope that he would reach headquarters an hour or so before the Administrator arrived by the mail-boat. If Bones could be trusted there would be no cause for worry. Bones should have the men's quarters whitewashed, the parade ground swept and garnished, and stores in excellent order for inspection, and all the books on hand for the Accountant-General to glance over.

But Bones!

Hamilton writhed internally at the thought of Francis Augustus and his inefficiency.

He had sent his second the most elaborate instructions, but if he knew his man, the languid Bones would do no more than pass those instructions on to a subordinate.

It was ten o'clock on the morning of the inspection that the *Zaire* came paddling furiously to the tiny concrete quay, and Hamilton gave a sigh of relief. For there, awaiting him, stood Lieutenant Tibbetts in the glory of his raiment— helmet sparkling white, steel hilt of sword a-glitter, khaki uniform, spotless and well-fitting.

"Mail-boat's just in, sir," Bones went on with unusual fierceness. "You're in time to meet His Excellency.

Stores all laid out, books in trim, parade ground and quarters whitewashed as per your jolly old orders, sir."

He saluted again, his eyes bulging, his face a veritable mask of ferocity, and, turning on his heel, he led the way to the beach.

"Here, hold hard!" said Hamilton; "what the dickens is the matter with you?"

"Seen the error of my ways, sir," growled Bones, again saluting punctiliously. "I've been an ass, sir—too lenient —given you a lot of trouble—shan't occur again."

There was not time to ask any further questions.

The two men had to run to reach the landing place in time, for the surf-boats were at that moment rolling to the yellow beach.

Sir Robert Sanleigh, in spotless white, was carried ashore, and his staff followed.

"Ah, Hamilton," said the great Bob, "everything all right?"

"Yes, your Excellency," said Hamilton, "there have been one or two serious killing palavers on which I will report."

Sir Robert nodded.

"You were bound to have a little trouble as soon as Sanders went," he said.

He was a methodical man and had little time for the work at hand, for the mail-boat was waiting to carry him to another station.   Books, quarters, and stores were in apple-pie order, and inwardly Hamilton raised his voice in praise of the young man who strode silently and fiercely by his side, his face still distorted with a new-found fierceness.

"The Houssas are all right, I suppose?" asked Sir Robert. "Discipline good—no crime?"

"The discipline is excellent, sir," replied Hamilton, heartily, "and we haven't had any serious crime for years."

Sir Robert Sanleigh fixed his *pince-nez* upon his nose and looked round the parade ground.   A dozen Houssas in two ranks stood at attention in the centre.

"Where are the rest of your men?" asked the Administrator.

"In gaol, sir." It was Bones who answered the question. Hamilton gasped.

"In gaol—I'm sorry—but I knew nothing of this. I've just arrived from the interior, your Excellency."

They walked across to the little party.

"Where is Sergeant Abiboo?" asked Hamilton suddenly.

"In gaol, sir," said Bones, promptly, "sentenced to death —scratchin' his leg on parade after bein' warned repeatedly by me to give up the disgusting habit."

"Where is Corporal Ahmet, Bones?" asked the frantic Hamilton.

"In gaol, sir," said Bones. "I gave him twenty years for talkin' in the ranks an' cheekin' me when I told him to shut up. There's a whole lot of them, sir," he went on casually. "I sentenced two chaps to death for fightin' in the lines, an' gave another feller ten years for——"

"I think that will do," said Sir Robert, tactfully. "A most excellent inspection, Captain Hamilton—now, I think, I'll get back to my ship."

He took Hamilton aside on the beach.

"What did you call that young man?" he asked.

"Bones, your Excellency," said Hamilton miserably.

"I should call him Blood and Bones," smiled His Excellency, as he shook hands.

* * * * *

"What's the good of bullyin' me, dear old chap?" asked Bones indignantly. "If I let a chap off, I'm kicked, an' if I punish him I'm kicked—it's enough to make a feller give up bein' judicial——"

"Bones, you're a goop," said Hamilton, in despair.

"A goop, sir?—if you'd be kind enough to explain——?"

"There's an ass," said Hamilton, ticking off one finger;

"and there's a silly ass," he ticked off the second; "and there's a silly ass who is such a silly ass that he doesn't know what a silly ass he is: we call him a goop."

"Thank you, sir," said Bones, without resentment, "and which is the goop, you or——"

Hamilton dropped his hand on his revolver butt, and for a moment there was murder in his eyes.

CHAPTER III

THE LOST N'BOSINI

"M'ILITANI, there is a bad palaver in the N'bosini country," said the gossip-chief of the Lesser Isisi, and wagged his head impressively.

Hamilton of the Houssas rose up from his camp chair and stretched himself to his full six feet. His laughing eyes— terribly blue they looked in the mahogany setting of his lean face—quizzed the chief, and his clean-shaven lips twitched ever so slightly.

Chief Idigi looked at him curiously. Idigi was squat and fat, but wise. None the less he gossiped, for, as they say on the river, "Even the wise *oochiri* is a chatterer."

"O, laughing Lord," said Idigi, almost humble in his awe—for blue eyes in a brown face are a great sign of devilry, "this is no smiling palaver, for they say——"

"Idigi," interrupted Hamilton, "I smile when you speak of the N'bosini, because there is no such land. Even Sandi, who has wisdom greater than *ju-ju*, he says that there is no N'bosini, but that it is the foolish talk of men who cannot see whence come their troubles and must find a land and a people and a king out of their mad heads. Go back to your village, Idigi, telling all men that I sit here for a spell in the place of my lord Sandi, and if there be, not one king of N'bosini, but a score, and if he lead, not one army, but three and three and three, I will meet him with my soldiers and he shall go the way of the bad king."

Idigi, unconvinced, shaking his head, said a doubtful "*Wa!*" and would continue upon his agreeable subject—for he was a lover of ghosts.

"Now," said he, impressively, "it is said that on the night before the moon came, there was seen, on the edge of the lake-forest, ten warriors of the N'bosini, with spears of fire and arrows tipped with stars, also——"

"Go to the devil!" said Hamilton, cheerfully. "The palaver is finished."

Later, he watched Idigi—so humble a man that he never travelled with more than four paddlers—winding his slow way up stream—and Hamilton was not laughing.

He went back to his canvas chair before the Residency, and sat for half an hour, alternately pinching and rubbing his bare arms—he was in his shirt sleeves—in a reverie which was not pleasant.

Here Lieutenant Augustus Tibbetts, returning from an afternoon's fishing, with a couple of weird-looking fish as his sole catch, found him and would have gone on with a little salute.

"Bones!" called Hamilton, softly.

Bones swung round. "Sir!" he said stiffly.

"Come off your horse, Bones," coaxed Hamilton.

"Not me," replied Bones; "I've finished with you, dear old fellow; as an officer an' a gentleman you've treated me rottenly—you have, indeed. Give me an order—I'll obey it. Tell me to lead a forlorn hope or go to bed at ten—I'll carry out instructions accordin' to military law, but outside of duty you're a jolly old rotter. I'm hurt, Ham, doocidly hurt. I think——"

"Oh shut up and sit down!" interrupted his chief, irritably. "You jaw and jaw till my head aches."

Reluctantly Lieutenant Tibbetts walked back, depositing his catch with the greatest care on the ground.

"What on earth have you got there?" asked Hamilton, curiously.

"I don't know whether it's cod or turbot," said the cautious Bones, "but I'll have 'em cooked and find out."

Hamilton grinned. "To be exact, they're catfish, and poisonous," he said, and whistled his orderly. "Oh, Ahmet," he said in Arabic, "take these fish and throw them away."

Bones fixed his monocle, and his eyes followed his catch till they were out of sight.

"Of course, sir," he said with resignation, "if you like to commandeer my fish it's not for me to question you."

"I'm a little worried, Bones," began Hamilton.

"A conscience sir," said Bones, smugly, "is a pretty rotten thing for a feller to have. I remember years ago——"

"There's a little unrest up there"—Hamilton waved his hand towards the dark green forest, sombre in the shadows of the evening—"a palaver I don't quite get the hang of. If I could only trust you, Bones!"

Lieutenant Tibbetts rose. He readjusted his monocle and stiffened himself to attention—a heroic pose which invariably accompanied his protests. But Hamilton gave him no opportunity.

"Anyway, I have to trust you, Bones," he said, "whether I like it or not. You get ready to clear out. Take twenty men and patrol the river between the Isisi and the Akasava."

In as few words as possible he explained the legend of the N'bosini. "Of course, there is no such place," he said; "it is a mythical land like the lost Atlantis—the home of the mysterious and marvellous tribes, populated by giants and filled with all the beautiful products of the world."

"I know, sir," said Bones, nodding his head. "It is like one of those building estate advertisements you read in the American papers: Young-man-go-west-an'-buy-Dudville Corner Blocks——"

"You have a horrible mind," said Hamilton. "However, get ready. I will have steam in the *Zaire* against your departure."

"There is one thing I should like to ask you about," said Bones, standing hesitatingly first on one leg and then on the other. "I think I have told you before that I have tickets in a Continental sweepstake. I should be awfully obliged——"

"Go away!" snarled Hamilton.

Bones went cheerfully enough.

He loved the life on the *Zaire*, the comfort of Sanders' cabin, the electric reading-lamp and the fine sense of authority. He would stand upon the bridge for hours, with folded arms and impassive face, staring ahead as the oily waters moved slowly under the bow of the stern-wheeler. Now and again he would turn to give a fierce order to the steersman or to the patient Yoka, the squat black *Krooman* who knew every inch of the river, and who stood all the time, his hand upon the lever of the telegraph ready to "slow" at the first sign of a new sandbank.

For, in parts, the river was less than two or three feet deep and the bed was constantly changing. The sounding boys, who stood on the bow of the steamer, whirling their long canes and singing the depth monotonously, would shout a warning cry, but long before their lips had framed a caution, Yoka would have pulled the telegraph over to "stop." His eyes would have detected the tiny ripple on the waters ahead which denoted a new "bank."

To Bones, the river was a deep, clear stream. He had no idea as to the depth and never troubled to inquire. These short, stern orders of his that he barked to left and right from time to time, nobody took the slightest notice of, and Bones would have been considerably embarrassed if they had. Observing that the steamer was tacking from shore to shore, a proceeding which, to Bones' orderly mind, seemed inconsistent with the dignity of the Government boat, he asked the reason.

"Lord," said the steersman, one Ebibi, "there are many banks hereabout, large sands, which silt up in a night, therefore we must make a passage for the *puc-a-puc*, by going from shore to shore."

"You're a silly ass," said Bones, "and let it go at that."

Yet, for all his irresponsibility, for all his wild and un-knowledgeable conspectus of the land and its people, there was instilled in the heart of Lieutenant Tibbetts something of the spirit of dark romance and adventure-loving, which association with the Coast alone can bring.

In the big house at Dorking where he had spent his child-hood, the ten-acre estate, where his father had lorded (himself a one-time Commissioner), he had watered the seed of desire which heredity had irradicably sown in his bosom; a desire not to be shaped by words, or confirmed in phrase, but best described as the discovery-lust, which sends men into dark, unknown places of the world to joyously sacrifice life and health that their names might be associated with some scrap of sure fact for the better guidance of unborn generations.

Bones was a dreamer of dreams.

On the bridge of the *Zaire* he was a Nelson taking the *Victory* into action, a Stanley, a Columbus, a Sir Garnet Wolseley forcing the passages of the Nile.

Small wonder that he turned from time to time to the steersman with a sharp "Put her to starboard," or "Port your helm a little."

Less wonder that the wholly uncomprehending steersman went on with his work as though Bones had no separate or tangible existence.

On the fourth evening after leaving headquarters, Bones summoned to his cabin Mahomet Ali, the sergeant in charge of his soldiers.

"O, Mahomet," said he, "tell me of this N'bosini of which men speak, and in which all native people believe, for my lord M'ilitani has said that there is no such place and that it is the dream of mad people."

"Master, that I also believe," said Mahomet Ali; "these people of the river are barbarians, having no God and being foredoomed for all time to hell, and it is my belief that his idea of N'bosini is no more than the Paradise of the faithful, of which the barbarians have heard and converted in their wild way."

"Tell me, who talks of N'bosini," said Bones, crossing his legs and leaning back in his chair, his hands behind his head; "for, remember that I am a stranger amongst you, Mahomet Ali, coming from a far land and having seen such marvels as——"

He paused, seeking the Arabic for "gramophone" and "motor-bus," then he went on wisely: "Such marvels as you cannot imagine."

"This I know of N'bosini," said the sergeant, "that all men along this river believe in it; all save Bosambo of the Ochori, who, as is well known, believes in nothing, since he is a follower of the Prophet and the one God."

Mahomet Ali salaamed devoutly.

"And men say that this land lies at the back of the N'gombi country; and others that it lies near the territories of the old King; and some others who say that it is a far journey beyond the French's territory, farther than man can walk, that its people have wings upon their shoulders and can fly, and that their eyes are so fierce that trees burn when they look upon them. This only we know, lord, we, of your soldiers, who have followed Sandi through all his high adventures, that when men talk of N'bosini, there is trouble, for they are seeking something to excuse their own wickedness."

All night long, as Bones turned from side to side in his hot cabin, listening to the ineffectual buzzings of the flies that sought, unsuccessfully, to reach the interior of the cabin through a fine-meshed screen, the problem of N'bosini revolved in his mind.

Was it likely, thought Bones, cunningly, that men should invent a country, even erring men, seeking an excuse? Did not all previous experience go to the support of the theory that N'bosini had some existence? In other words that, planted in the secret heart of some forest in the territory, barred from communication with the world by swift rivers of the high tangle of forests, there was, in being, a secret tribe of which only rumours had been heard—a tribe of white men, perhaps!

Bones had read of such things in books; he knew his *Solomon's Mines* and was well acquainted with his *Allan Quatermain*. Who knows but that through the forest was a secret path held, perchance, by armoured warriors, which led to the mountains at the edge of the Old King's territory, in the folds of the inaccessible hills, there might be a city of stone, peopled and governed by stern white-bearded men, and streets filled with beautiful maidens garbed in the style of ancient Greece!

"It is all dam' nonsense of course," said Bones to himself, though feebly; "but, after all there may be something in this. There's no smoke without fire."

The idea took hold of him and gripped him most powerfully. He took Sanders' priceless maps and carefully triangulated them, consulting every other written authority on the ship. He stopped at villages and held palavers on this question of N'bosini and acquired a whole mass of conflicting information.

If you smile at Bones, you smile at the glorious spirit of enterprise which has created Empire. Out of such dreams as ran criss-cross through the mind of Lieutenant Tibbetts there have arisen nationalities undreamt of and Empires Cæsar never knew.

Now one thing is certain, that Bones, in pursuing his inquiries about N'bosini, was really doing a most useful piece of work.

The palavers he called had a deeper significance to the men who attended them than purely geographical inquiries. Thus, the folk of the Isisi planning a little raid upon certain Akasava fishermen, who had established themselves unlawfully upon the Isisi river-line, put away their spears and folded their hands when N'bosini was mentioned, because Bones was unconsciously probing their excuse before they advanced it.

Idigi, himself, who, in his caution, had prepared Hamilton for some slight difference of opinion between his own tribe and the N'gombi of the interior, read into the earnest inquiries of Lieutenant Tibbetts, something more than a patient spirit of research.

All that Hamilton had set his subordinate to accomplish Bones was doing, though none was more in ignorance of the fact than himself, and, since all men owed a grudge to the Ochori, palavers, which had as their object an investigation into the origin of the N'bosini legend, invariably ended in the suggestion rather than the statement that the only authority upon this mysterious land, and the still more mysterious tribe who inhabited it, was Bosambo of the Ochori. Thus, subtly, was Bosambo saddled with all responsibility in the matter.

Hamilton's parting injunction to Bones had been:

"Be immensely civil to Bosambo, because he is rather sore with you and he is a very useful man."

Regarding him, as he did, as the final authority upon the N'bosini, Bones made elaborate preparations to carry out his chief's commands. He came round the river bend to the Ochori city, with flags fluttering at his white mast, with his soldiers drawn up on deck, with his buglers tootling, and his siren sounding, and Bosambo, ever ready to jump to the conclusion that he was being honoured for his own sake, found that this time, at least, he had made no mistake and rose to the occasion.

In an emerald-green robe with twelve sock suspenders strapped about his legs and dangling tags aglitter—he had bought these on his visit to the Coast—with an umbrella of state and six men carrying a canopy over his august person, he came down to the beach to greet the representatives of the Government.

"Lord," said Bosambo humbly, "it gives me great pride that your lordship should bring his beautiful presence to my country. All this month I have sat in my hut, wondering why you came not to the Ochori, and I have not eaten food for many days because of my sorrow and my fear that you would not come to us."

Bones walked under the canopy to the chief's hut. A superior palaver occupied the afternoon on the question of taxation. Here Bones was on safe ground. Having no power to remit taxes, but having most explicit instructions from his chief, which admitted of no compromise, it was an easy matter for Bones to shake his head and say in English:

"Nothin' doing"; a phrase which, afterwards, passed into the vocabulary of the Ochori as the equivalent of denial of privilege.

It was on the second day that Bones broached the question of the N'bosini. Bosambo had it on the tip of his tongue to deny all knowledge of this tribe, was even preparing to call down destruction upon the heads of the barbarians who gave credence to the story. Then he asked curiously:

"Lord, why do you speak of the land or desire knowledge upon it?"

"Because," said Bones, firmly, "it is in mind, Bosambo, that somewhere in this country, dwell such a people, and since all men agree that you are wise, I have come to you to seek it."

"*O ko*," said Bosambo, under his breath.

He fixed his eyes upon Bones, licked his lips a little, twiddled his fingers a great deal, and began:

"Lord, it is written in a certain *Suru* that wisdom comest from the East, and that knowledge from the West, that courage comes from the North, and sin from the South."

"Steady the Buffs, Bosambo!" murmured Bones, reprovingly, "I come from the South."

He spoke in English, and Bosambo, resisting the temptation to retort in an alien tongue, and realising perhaps that he would need all the strength of his more extensive vocabulary to convince his hearer, continued in Bomongo:

"Now I tell you," he went on solemnly, "if Sandi had come, Sandi, who loves me better than his brother, and who knew my father and lived with him for many years, and if Sandi spoke to me, saying 'Tell me, O Bosambo, where is N'bosini?' I answer 'Lord, there are things which are written and which I know cannot be told, not even to you whom I love so dearly.'" He paused.

Bones was impressed. He stared, wide-eyed, at the chief, tilted his helmet back a little from his damp brow, folded his hands on his knees and opened his mouth a little.

"But it is you, O my lord," said Bosambo, extravagantly, "who asks this question. You, who have suddenly come amongst us and who are brighter to us than the moon and dearer to us than the land which grows corn; therefore must I speak to you that which is in my heart. If I lie, strike me down at your feet, for I am ready to die."

He paused again, throwing out his arms invitingly, but Bones said nothing.

"Now this I tell you," Bosambo shook his finger impressively, "that the N'bosini lives."

"Where?" asked Bones, quickly.

Already he saw himself lecturing before a crowded audience at the Royal Geographical Society, his name in the papers, perhaps a Tibbett River or a Francis Augustus Mountain added to the sum of geographical knowledge.

"It is in a certain place," said Bosambo, solemnly, "which only I know, and I have sworn a solemn oath by many sacred things which I dare not break, by letting of blood and by rubbing in of salt, that I will not divulge the secret."

"O, tell me, Bosambo," demanded Bones, leaning forward and speaking rapidly, "what manner of people are they who live in the city of N'bosini?"

"They are men and women," said Bosambo after a pause.

"White or black?" asked Bones, eagerly.

Bosambo thought a little.

"White," he said soberly, and was immensely pleased at the impression he created.

"I thought so," said Bones, excitedly, and jumped up, his eyes wider than ever, his hands trembling as he pulled his note-book from his breast pocket.

"I will make a book[1] of this, Bosambo," he said, almost incoherently. "You shall speak slowly, telling me all things, for I must write in English."

He produced his pencil, squatted again, open book upon his knee, and looked up at Bosambo to commence.

"Lord, I cannot do this," said Bosambo, his face heavy with gloom, "for have I not told your lordship that I have sworn such oath? Moreover," he said carelessly, "we who know the secret, have each hidden a large bag of silver in the ground, all in one place, and we have sworn that he who tells the secret shall lose his share. Now, by the Prophet, 'Eye-of-the-Moon' (this was one of the names which Bones had earned, for which his monocle was responsible), I cannot do this thing."

"How large was this bag, Bosambo?" asked Bones, nibbling at the end of his pencil.

"Lord, it was so large," said Bosambo.

[1]"Book" means any written thing. A note is a book.

He moved his hands outward slowly, keeping his eyes fixed upon Lieutenant Tibbetts till he read in them a hint of pain and dismay. Then he stopped.

"So large," he said, choosing the dimensions his hands had indicated before Bones showed signs of alarm. "Lord, in the bag was silver worth a hundred English pounds."

Bones, continuing his meal of cedar-wood, thought the matter out.

It was worth it.

"Is it a large city?" he asked suddenly.

"Larger than the whole of the Ochori," answered Bosambo impressively.

"And tell me this, Bosambo, what manner of houses are these which stand in the city of the N'bosini?"

"Larger than kings' huts," said Bosambo.

"Of stone?"

"Lord, of rock, so that they are like mountains," replied Bosambo.

Bone shut his book and got up.

"This day I go back to M'ilitani, carrying word of the N'bosini," said he, and Bosambo's jaw dropped, though Bones did not notice the fact.

"Presently I will return, bringing with me silver of the value of a hundred English pounds, and you shall lead us to this strange city."

"Lord, it is a far way," faltered Bosambo, "across many swamps and over high mountains; also there is much sickness and death, wild beasts in the forests and snakes in the trees and terrible storms of rain."

"Nevertheless, I will go," said Bones, in high spirits, "I, and you also."

"Master," said the agitated Bosambo, "say no word of this to M'ilitani; if you do, be sure that my enemies will discover it and I shall be killed."

Bones hesitated and Bosambo pushed his advantage.

"Rather, lord," said he, "give me all the silver you have, and let me go alone, carrying a message to the mighty chief of the N'bosini. Presently I will return, bringing with me strange news, such as no white lord, not even Sandi, has received or heard, and cunning weapons which only N'bosini use and strange magics. Also will I bring you stories of their river, but I will go alone, though I die, for what am I that I should deny myself from the service of your lordship?"

It happened that Bones had some twenty pounds on the *Zaire*, and Bosambo condescended to come aboard to accept, with outstretched hands, this earnest of his master's faith.

"Lord," said he, solemnly, as he took a farewell of his benefactor, "though I lose a great bag of silver because I have betrayed certain men, yet I know that, upon a day to come, you will pay me all that I desire. Go in peace."

It was a hilarious, joyous, industrious Bones who went down the river to headquarters, occupying his time in writing diligently upon large sheets of foolscap in his no less large unformed handwriting, setting forth all that Bosambo had told him, and all the conclusions he might infer from the confidence of the Ochori king.

He was bursting with his news. At first, he had to satisfy his chief that he had carried out his orders.

Fortunately, Hamilton needed little convincing; his own spies had told him of the quietening down of certain truculent sections of his unruly community and he was prepared to give his subordinate all the credit that was due to him.

It was after dinner and the inevitable rice pudding had been removed and the pipes were puffing bluely in the big room of the Residency, when Bones unburdened himself.

"Sir," he began, "you think I am an ass."

"I was not thinking so at this particular moment," said Hamilton; "but, as a general concensus of my opinion concerning you, I have no fault to find with it."

"You think poor old Bones is a goop," said Lieutenant

Tibbetts with a pitying smile, "and yet the name of poor old Bones is going down to posterity, sir."

"That is posterity's look-out," said Hamilton, offensively; but Bones ignored the rudeness.

"You also imagine that there is no such land as the N'bosini, I think?"

Bones put the question with a certain insolent assurance which was very irritating.

"I not only think, but I know," replied Hamilton.

Bones laughed, a sardonic, knowing laugh.

"We shall see," he said, mysteriously; "I hope, in the course of a few weeks, to place a document in your possession that will not only surprise, but which, I believe, knowing that beneath a somewhat uncouth manner lies a kindly heart, will also please you."

"Are you chucking up the army?" asked Hamilton with interest.

"I have no more to say, sir," said Bones.

He got up, took his helmet from a peg on the wall, saluted and walked stiffly from the Residency and was swallowed up in the darkness of the parade ground.

A quarter of an hour later, there came a tap upon his door and Mahomet Ali, his sergeant, entered.

"Ah, Mah'met," said Hamilton, looking up with a smile, "all things were quiet on the river my lord Tibbetts tells me."

"Lord, everything was proper," said the sergeant, "and all people came to palaver humbly."

"What seek you now?" asked Hamilton.

"Lord," said Mahomet, "Bosambo of the Ochori is, as you know, of my faith, and by certain oaths we are as blood brothers. This happened after a battle in the year of Drought when Bosambo saved my life."

"All this I know," said Hamilton.

"Now, lord," said Mahomet Ali, "I bring you this."

He took from the inside of his uniform jacket a little canvas bag, opened it slowly and emptied its golden contents upon the table. There was a small shining heap of sovereigns and a twisted note; this latter he placed in Hamilton's hand and the Houssa captain unfolded it. It was a letter in Arabic in Bosambo's characteristic and angular handwriting.

"From Bosambo, the servant of the Prophet, of the upper river in the city of the Ochori, to M'ilitani, his master. Peace on your house.

"In the name of God I send you this news. My lord with the moon-eye, making inquiries about the N'bosini, came to the Ochori and I told him much that he wrote down in a book. Now, I tell you, M'ilitani, that I am not to blame, because my lord with the moon-eye wrote down these things. Also he gave me twenty English pounds because I told him certain stories and this I send to you, that you shall put it in with my other treasures, making a mark in your book that this twenty pounds is the money of Bosambo of the Ochori, and that you will send me a book, saying that this money has come to you and is safely in your hands. Peace and felicity upon your house.

"Written in my city of Ochori and given to my brother, Mahomet Ali, who shall carry it to M'ilitani at the mouth of the river."

"Poor old Bones!" said Hamilton, as he slowly counted the money. "Poor old Bones!" he repeated.

He took an account book from his desk and opened it at a page marked "Bosambo." His entry was significant.

To a long list of credits which ran:

Received £30. (Sale of Rubber.)
Received £25. (Sale of Gum.)
Received £130. (Sale of Ivory.)

he added:

Received £20. (Author's Fees.)

CHAPTER IV

THE FETISH STICK

N'GORI the Chief had a son who limped and lived. This was a marvellous thing in a land where cripples are severely discouraged and malformity is a sure passport for heaven.

The truth is that M'fosa was born in a fishing village at a period of time when all the energies of the Akasava were devoted to checking and defeating the predatory raidings of the N'gombi, under that warlike chief G'osimalino, who also kept other nations on the defensive, and held the river basin, from the White River, by the old king's territory, to as far south as the islands of the Lesser Isisi.

When M'fosa was three months old, Sanders had come with a force of soldiers, had hanged G'osimalino to a high tree, had burnt his villages and destroyed his crops and driven the remnants of his one-time invincible army to the little known recesses of the Itusi Forest.

Those were the days of the Cakitas or government chiefs, and it was under the beneficent sway of one of these that M'fosa grew to manhood, though many attempts were made to lure him to unfrequented waterways and blind crocodile creeks where a lame man might be lost, and no one be any the wiser.

Chief of the eugenists was Kobolo, the boy's uncle, and N'gori's own brother. This dissatisfied man, with several of M'fosa's cousins, once partially succeeded in kidnapping the lame boy, and they were on their way to certain middle islands in the broads of the river to accomplish their scheme —which was to put out the eyes of M'fosa and leave him to die—when Sanders had happened along.

He it was who set all the men of M'fosa's village to cut

down a high pine tree—at an infernal distance from the village, and had men working for a week, trimming and planing that pine; and another week they spent carrying the long stem through the forest (Sanders had devilishly chosen his tree in the most inaccessible part of the woods), and yet another week digging large holes and erecting it.

For he was a difficult man to please. Broad backs ran sweat to pull and push and hoist that great flagstaff (as it appeared with its strong pulley and smooth sides) to its place. And no sooner was it up than my lord Sandi had changed his mind and must have it in another place. Sanders would come back at intervals to see how the work was progressing. At last it was fixed, that monstrous pole, and the men of the village sighed thankfully.

"Lord, tell me," N'gori had asked, "why you put this great stick in the ground?"

"This," said Sanders, "is for him who injures M'fosa your son; upon this will I hang him. And if there be more men than one who take to the work of slaughter, behold! I will have yet another tree cut and hauled, and put in a place and upon that will I hang the other man. All men shall know this sign, the high stick, as my fetish; and it shall watch the evil hearts and carry me all thoughts, good and evil. And then I tell you, that such is its magic, that if needs be, it shall draw me from the end of the world to punish wrong."

This is the story of the fetish stick of the Akasava and of how it came to be in its place.

None did hurt to M'fosa, and he grew to be a man, and as he grew and his father became first counsellor, then petty chief, and, at last, paramount chief of the nation, M'fosa developed in hauteur and bitterness, for this high pole rainwashed, and sunburnt, was a reminder, not of the strong hand that had been stretched out to save him, but of his own infirmity.

82

And he came to hate it, and by some curious perversion to hate the man who had set it up.

Most curious of all to certain minds, he was the first of those who condemned, and secretly slew, the unfortunates, who either came into the world hampered by disfigurement, or who, by accident, were unfitted for the great battle.

He it was who drowned Kibusu the woodman, who lost three fingers by the slipping of the axe; he was the leader of the young men who fell upon the boy Sandilo-M'goma, who was crippled by fire; and though the fetish stood a menace to all, reading thoughts and clothed with authority, yet M'fosa defied spirits and went about his work reckless of consequence.

When Sanders had gone home, and it seemed that law had ceased to be, N'gori (as I have shown) became of a sudden a bold and fearless man, furbished up his ancient grievances and might have brought trouble to the land, but for a watchful Bosambo.

This is certain, however, that N'gori himself was a good-enough man at heart, and if there was evil in his actions be sure that behind him prompting, whispering, subtly threatening him, was his malignant son, a sinister figure with one eye half-closed, and a figure that went limping through the city with a twisted smile.

An envoy came to the Ochori country bearing green branches of the Isisi palm, which signifies peace, and at the head of the mission—for mission it was—came M'fosa.

"Lord Bosambo," said the man who limped, "N'gori, the chief, my father, has sent me, for he desires your friendship and help; also your loving countenance at his great feast."

"Oh, oh!" said Bosambo, dryly, "what king's feast is this?"

"Lord," rejoined the other, "it is no king's feast, but a great dance of rejoicing, for our crops are very plentiful, and our goats have multiplied more than a man can count;

83

therefore my father said: Go you to Bosambo of the Ochori, he who was once my enemy and now indeed my friend. And say to him 'Come into my city, that I may honour you.'"

Bosambo thought.

"How can your lord and father feast so many as I would bring?" he asked thoughtfully, as he sat, chin on palm, pondering the invitation, "for I have a thousand spearmen, all young men and fond of food."

M'fosa's face fell.

"Yet, Lord Bosambo," said he, "if you come without your spearmen, but with your counsellors only——"

Bosambo looked at the limper, through half-closed eyes. "I carry spears to a Dance of Rejoicing," he said significantly, "else I would not Dance or Rejoice."

M'fosa showed his teeth, and his eyes were filled with hateful fires. He left the Ochori with bad grace, and was lucky to leave it at all, for certain men of the country, whom he had put to torture (having captured them fishing in unauthorised waters), would have rushed him but for Bosambo's presence.

His other invitation was more successful. Hamilton of the Houssas was at the Isisi City when the deputation called upon him.

"Here's a chance for you, Bones," he said.

Lieutenant Tibbetts had spent a vain day, fishing in the river with a rod and line, and was sprawling upon a deck-chair under the awning of the bridge.

"Would you like to be the guest of honour at N'gori's little thanksgiving service?"

Bones sat up.

"Shall I have to make a speech?" he asked cautiously.

"You may have to respond for the ladies," said Hamilton. "No, my dear chap, all you will have to do will be to sit round and look clever."

Bones thought awhile.

84

"I'll bet you're putting me on to a rotten job," he accused, "but I'll go."

"I wish you would," said Hamilton, seriously. "I can't get the hang of M'fosa's mind, ever since you treated him with such leniency."

"If you're goin' to dig up the grisly past, dear old sir," said a reproachful Bones, "if you insist recalling events which I hoped, sir, were hidden in oblivion, I'm going to bed."

He got up, this lank youth, fixed his eyeglass firmly and glared at his superior.

"Sit down and shut up," said Hamilton, testily; "I'm not blaming you. And I'm not blaming N'gori. It's that son of his—listen to this."

He beckoned the three men who had come down from the Akasava as bearers of the invitation.

"Say again what your master desires," he said.

"Thus speaks N'gori, and I talk with his voice," said the spokesman, "that you shall cut down the devil-stick which Sandi planted in our midst, for it brings shame to us, and also to M'fosa the son of our master."

"How may I do this?" asked Hamilton, "I, who am but the servant of Sandi? For I remember well that he put the stick there to make a great magic."

"Now the magic is made," said the sullen headman; "for none of our people have died the death since Sandi set it up."

"And dashed lucky you've been," murmured Bones.

"Go back to your master and tell him this," said Hamilton. "Thus says M'ilitani, my lord Tibbetti will come on your feast day and you shall honour him; as for the stick, it stands till Sandi says it shall not stand. The palaver is finished."

He paced up and down the deck when the men had gone, his hands behind him, his brows knit in worry.

85

"Four times have I been asked to cut down Sanders' pole," he mused aloud. "I wonder what the idea is?"

"The idea?" said Bones, "the idea, my dear old silly old fellow, isn't it as plain as your dashed old nose? They don't want it!"

Hamilton looked down at him.

"What a brain you must have, Bones!" he said admiringly. "I often wonder you don't employ it."

II

By the Blue Pool in the forest there is a famous tree gifted with certain properties. It is known in the vernacular of the land, and I translate it literally, "The-tree-that-has-no-echo-and-eats-up-sound." Men believe that all that is uttered beneath its twisted branches may be remembered, but not repeated, and if one shouts in its deadening shade, even they who stand no farther than a stride from its furthermost stretch of branch or leaf, will hear nothing.

Therefore is the Silent Tree much in favour for secret palaver, such as N'gori and his limping son attended, and such as the Lesser Isisi came to fearfully.

N'gori, who might be expected to take a very leading part in the discussion which followed the meeting, was, in fact, the most timorous of those who squatted in the shadow of the huge cedar.

Full of reservations, cautions, doubts and counsels of discretion was N'gori till his son turned on him, grinning as was his wont when in his least pleasant mood.

"O, my father," said he softly, "they say on the river that men who die swiftly say no more than 'wait' with their last breath; now I tell you that all my young men who plot secretly with me, are for chopping you—but because I am like a god to them, they spare you."

"My son," said N'gori uneasily, "this is a very high

86

palaver, for many chiefs have risen and struck at the Government, and always Sandi has come with his soldiers, and there have been backs that have been sore for the space of a moon, and necks that have been sore for this time," he snapped his fingers, "and then have been sore no more."

"Sandi has gone," said M'fosa.

"Yet his fetish stands," insisted the old man; "all day and all night his dreadful spirit watches us; for this we have all seen that the very lightnings of M'shimba M'shamba run up that stick and do it no harm.   Also M'ilitani and Moon-in-the-Eye——"

"They are fools," a counsellor broke in.

"Lord M'ilitani is no fool, this I know," interrupted a fourth.

"Tibbetti comes—and brings no soldiers.   Now I tell you my mind that Sandi's fetish is dead—as Sandi has passed from us, and this is the sign I desire—I and my young men. We shall make a killing palavar in the face of the killing stick, and if Sandi lives and has not lied to us, he shall come from the end of the world as he said."

He rose up from the ground.   There was no doubt now who ruled the Akasava.

"The palaver is finished," he said, and led the way back to the city, his father meekly following in the rear.

Two days later Bones arrived at the city of the Akasava, bringing with him no greater protection than a Houssa orderly afforded.

III

On a certain night in September Mr. Commissioner Sanders was the guest of the Colonial Secretary at his country seat in Berkshire.

Sanders, who was no society man, either by training or by inclination, would have preferred wandering aimlessly about the brilliantly lighted streets of London, but the engagement was a long-standing one. In a sense he was a lion against his will. His name was known, people had written of his character and his sayings; he had even, to his own amazement, delivered a lecture before the members of the Ethnological Society on "Native Folk-lore," and had emerged from the ordeal triumphantly. The guests of Lord Castleberry found Sanders a shy, silent man who could not be induced to talk of the land he loved so dearly. They might have voted him a bore, but for the fact that he so completely effaced himself they had little opportunity for forming so definite a judgment.

It was on the second night of his visit to Newbury Grange that they had cornered him in the billiard-room. It was the beautiful daughter of Lord Castleberry who, with the audacity of youth, forced him, metaphorically speaking, into a corner, from whence there was no escape.

"We've been very patient, Mr. Sanders," she pouted; "we are all dying to hear of your wonderful country, and Bosambo, and fetishes and things, and you haven't said a word."

"There is little to say," he smiled; "perhaps if I told you —something about fetishes. . . .?"

There was a chorus of approval.

Sanders had gained enough courage from his experience before the Ethnological Society, and began to talk.

"Wait," said Lady Betty; "let's have all these glaring lights out—they limit our imagination."

There was a click, and, save for one bracket light behind Sanders, the room was in darkness. He was grateful to the girl, and well rewarded her and the party that sat round on chairs, on benches around the edge of the billiard-table, listening. He told them stories . . . curious, unbelievable; of ghost palavers, of strange rites, of mysterious messages carried across the great space of forests.

"Tell us about fetishes," said the girl's voice.

88

Sanders smiled. There rose to his eyes the spectacle of a hot and weary people bringing in a giant tree through the forest, inch by inch.

And he told the story of the fetish of the Akasava.

"And I said," he concluded, "that I would come from the end of the world——"

He stopped suddenly and stared straight ahead. In the faint light they saw him stiffen like a setter.

"What is wrong?"

Lord Castleberry was on his feet, and somebody clicked on the lights.

But Sanders did not notice.

He was looking towards the end of the room, and his face was set and hard.

"O, M'fosa," he snarled, "O, dog!"

They heard the strange staccato of the Bomongo tongue and wondered.

Lieutenant Tibbetts, helmetless, his coat torn, his lip bleeding, offered no resistance when they strapped him to the smooth high pole. Almost at his feet lay the dead Houssa orderly whom M'fosa had struck down from behind.

In a wide circle, their faces half revealed by the crackling fire which burnt in the centre, the people of the Akasava city looked on impressively.

N'gori, the chief, his brows all wrinkled in terror, his shaking hands at his mouth in a gesture of fear, was no more than a spectator, for his masterful son limped from side to side, consulting his counsellors.

Presently the men who had bound Bones stepped aside, their work completed, and M'fosa came limping across to his prisoners.

"Now," he mocked. "Is it hard for you this fetish stick which Sandi has placed?"

"You're a low cad," said Bones, dropping into English in his wrath. "You're a low, beastly bounder, an' I'm simply disgusted with you."

"What does he say?" they asked M'fosa.

"He speaks to his gods in his own tongue," answered the limper; "for he is greatly afraid."

Lieutenant Tibbets went on:

"Hear," said he in fluent and vitriolic Bomongo—for he was using that fisher dialect which he knew so much better than the more sonorous tongue of the Upper River—"O hear, eater of fish, O lame dog, O nameless child of a monkey!"

M'fosa's lips went up one-sidedly.

"Lord," said he softly, "presently you shall say no more, for I will cut your tongue out that you shall be lame of speech . . . afterwards I will burn you and the fetish stick, so that you all tumble together."

"Be sure you will tumble into hell," said Bones cheerfully, "and that quickly, for you have offended Sandi's Ju-ju, which is powerful and terrible."

If he could gain time—time for some miraculous news to come to Hamilton, who, blissfully unconscious of the treachery to his second-in-command, was sleeping twenty miles downstream—unconscious, too, of the Akasava fleet of canoes which was streaming towards his little steamer.

Perhaps M'fosa guessed his thoughts.

"You die alone, Tibbetti," he said, "though I planned a great death for you, with Bosambo at your side; and in the matter of ju-jus, behold! you shall call for Sandi—whilst you have a tongue."

He took from the raw-hide sheath that was strapped to the calf of his bare leg, a short N'gombi knife, and drew it along the palm of his hand.

"Call now, O Moon-in-the-Eye!" he scoffed.

Bones saw the horror and braced himself to meet it.

"O Sandi!" cried M'fosa, "O planter of ju-ju, come quickly!"

"Dog!"

M'fosa whipped round, the knife dropping from his hand.

He knew the voice, was paralysed by the concentrated malignity in the voice.

There stood Sandi—not half a dozen paces from him.

A Sandi in strange black clothing, with a big white-breasted shirt . . . but Sandi, hard-eyed and threatening.

"Lord, lord!" he stammered, and put up his hands to his eyes.

He looked again—the figure had vanished.

"Magic!" he mumbled, and lurched forward in terror and hate to finish his work.

Then through the crowd stalked a tall man.

A rope of monkey's tails covers one broad shoulder, his left arm and hand were hidden by an oblong shield of hide.

In one hand he held a slim throwing spear and this he balanced delicately.

"I am Bosambo of the Ochori," he said magnificently and unnecessarily; "you sent for me and I have come—bringing a thousand spears."

M'fosa blinked, but said nothing.

"On the river," Bosambo went on, "I met many canoes that went to a killing—behold!"

It was the head of M'fosa's lieutenant, who had charge of the surprise party.

For a moment M'fosa looked, then turned to leap, and Bosambo's spear caught him in mid-air.

"Jolly old Bosambo!" muttered Bones, and fainted.

* * * *

Four thousand miles away Sanders was offering his apologies to a startled company.

"I could have sworn I saw—something," he said, and he told no more stories that night.

91

CHAPTER V

A FRONTIER AND A CODE

To understand this story you must know that at one point of Ochori borderline, the German, French, and Belgian territories shoot three narrow tongues that form, roughly, the segments of a half-circle. Whether the German tongue is split in the middle by N'glili River, so that it forms a flattened broad arrow, with the central prong the river is a moot point. We, in Downing Street, claim that the lower angle of this arrow is wholly ours, and that all the flat basin of the Field of Blood (as they call it) is entitled to receive the shadow which a flapping Union Jack may cast.

If Downing Street were to send that frantic code-wire to "Polonius" to Hamilton in these days he could not obey the instructions, for reasons which I will give. As a matter of fact the code has now been changed, Lieutenant Tibbetts being mainly responsible for the alteration.

Hamilton, in his severest mood, wrote a letter to Bones, and it is worth reproducing.

That Bones was living a dozen yards from Captain Hamilton, and that they shared a common mess-table, adds rather than distracts from the seriousness of the correspondence. The letter ran:

"The Residency,
"September 24th.

"From Officer commanding Houssas detachment Headquarters, to Officer commanding "B" company of Houssas.

"Sir,—

"I have the honour to direct your attention to that paragraph of King's regulations which directs that an officer's sole attention should be concentrated upon executing the lawful commands of his superior.

"I have had occasion recently to correct a certain tendency on your part to employing War Department property and the servants of the Crown for your own special use. I need hardly point out to you that such conduct on your part is subversive to discipline and directly contrary to the spirit and letter of regulations. More especially would I urge the impropriety of utilizing government telegraph lines for the purpose of securing information regarding your gambling transactions. Matters have now reached a very serious crisis, and I feel sure that you will see the necessity for refraining from these breaches of discipline.

"I have the honour to be, sir,
"Your obedient servant,
"P. G. HAMILTON, 'Captain.'"

When two white men, the only specimen of their race and class within a radius of hundreds of miles, are living together in an isolated post, they either hate or tolerate one another. The exception must always be found in two men of a similar service having similar objects to gain, and infused with a common spirit of endeavour.

Fortunately neither Lieutenant Tibbetts nor his superior were long enough associated to get upon one another's nerves.

Lieutenant Tibbetts received this letter while he was shaving, and came across the parade ground outrageously attired in his pyjamas and his helmet. Clambering up the wooden stairs, his slippers flap-flapping across the broad verandah, he burst into the chief's bedroom interrupting a stern and frigid Captain Hamilton in the midst of his early morning coffee and roll.

"Look here, old sport," said Bones, indignantly waving a frothy shaving-brush at the other, "what the dooce is all this about?"

He displayed a crumpled letter.

"Lieutenant Tibbetts," said Hamilton of the Houssas severely, "have you no sense of decency?"

93

"Sense of decency, my dear old thing!" repeated Bones. "I am simply full of it. That is why I have come."

A terrible sight was Bones at that early hour with the open pyjama jacket showing his scraggy neck, with his fish mouth drooping dismally, his round, staring eyes and his hair rumpled up, one frantic tuft at the back standing up in isolation.

Hamilton stared at him, and it was the stern stare of a disciplinarian. But Bones was not to be put out of countenance by so small a thing as an icy glance.

"There is no sense in getting peevish with me, old Ham," he said, squatting down on the nearest chair; "this is what I call a stupid, officious, unnecessary letter. Why this haughtiness? Why these crushing inferences? Why this unkindness to poor old Bones?"

"The fact of it is, Bones," said Hamilton, accepting the situation, "you are spending too much of your time in the telegraph station."

Bones got up slowly.

"Captain Hamilton, sir!" he said reproachfully, "after all I have done for you."

"Beyond selling me one of your beastly sweepstake tickets for five shillings," said Hamilton, unpleasantly, "a ticket which I dare say you have taken jolly good care will not win a prize, I fail to see in what manner you have helped me. Now, Bones, you will have to pay more attention to your work. There is no sense in slacking; we will have Sanders back here before we know where we are, and when he starts nosing round there will be a lot of trouble. Besides, you are shirking."

"Me!" gasped Bones, outraged. "Me—shirking? You forget yourself, sir!"

Even Bones could not be dignified with a lather brush in one hand and a half-shaven cheek, testifying to the hastiness of his departure from his quarters.

"I only wish to say, sir," said Bones, "that during the period I have had the honour to serve under your command I have settled possibly more palavers of a distressingly ominous character than the average Commissioner is called upon to settle in the course of a year."

"As you have created most of the palavers yourself," said Hamilton, unkindly, "I do not deny this. In other words, you have got yourself into more tangles, and you've had to crawl out more often."

"It is useless appealing to your better nature, sir," said Bones.

He saluted with the hand that held the lather brush, turned about like an automaton, tripped over the mat, recovered himself with an effort, and preserving what dignity a man can preserve in pink-striped pyjamas and a sun helmet, stalked majestically back to his quarters. Half-way across he remembered something and came doubling back, clattering into Hamilton's room unceremoniously.

"There is one thing I forgot to say," he said, "about those sweepstake tickets. If I happen to be killed on any future expedition that you may send me, you will understand that the whole of my movable property is yours, absolutely. And I may add, sir," he said at the doorway with one hand on the lintel ready to execute a strategic flank movement out of range, "that with this legacy I offer you my forgiveness for the perfectly beastly time you have given me. Good morning, sir."

There was a commanding officer's parade of Houssas at noon. It was not until he stalked across the square and clicked his heels together as he reported the full strength of his company present that Hamilton saw his subordinate again.

The parade over, Bones went huffily to his quarters.

He was hurt. To be told he had been shirking his duty touched a very tender and sensitive spot of his.

In preparation for the movement which he had expected

95

to make he had kept his company on the move for a fort-night. For fourteen terrible days in all kinds of weather, he had worked like a native in the forest; with sham fights and blank cartridge attacks upon imaginary positions, with scaling of stockades and building of bridges—all work at which his soul revolted—to be told at the end he had shirked his work!

Certainly he had come down to headquarters more often perhaps than was necessary, but then he was properly interested in the draw of a continental sweepstake which might, with any kind of luck, place him in the possession of a considerable fortune. Hamilton was amiable at lunch, even communicative at dinner, and for him rather serious.

For if the truth be told he was desperately worried. The cause was, as it had often been with Sanders, that French-German-Belgian territory which adjoins the Ochori country. All the bad characters, not only the French of the Belgian Congo, but of the badly-governed German lands—all the tax resisters, the murderers, and the criminals of every kind, but the lawless contingents of every nation, formed a floating nomadic population in the tree-covered hills which lay beyond the country governed by Bosambo.

Of late there had been a larger break-away than usual. A strong force of rebellious natives was reported to be within a day's march of the Ochori boundary. This much Hamilton knew. But he had known of such occurrences before; not once, but a score of times had alarming news come from the French border.

He had indeed made many futile trips into the heart of the Ochori country.

Forced marches through little known territory, and long and tiring waits for the invader that never came, had dulled his senses of apprehension. He had to take a chance. The Administrator's office would warn him from time to time, and ask him conventionally to make his arrangements to meet all contingencies and Sanders would as conventionally reply that the condition of affairs on the Ochori border was engaging his most earnest attention.

"What is the use of worrying about it now?" asked Bones at dinner.

Hamilton shook his head.

"There was a certain magic in old Sanders' name," he said.

Bones' lips pursed.

"My dear old chap," he said, "there is a bit of magic in mine."

"I have not noticed it," said Hamilton.

"I am getting awfully popular as a matter of fact," said Bones complacently. "The last time I was up the river, Bosambo came ten miles down stream to meet me and spend the day."

"Did you lose anything?" asked Hamilton ungraciously.

Bones thought.

"Now you come to mention it," he said slowly, "I did lose quite a lot of things, but dear old Bosambo wouldn't play a dirty trick on a pal. I know Bosambo."

"If there is one thing more evident than another," said Hamilton, "it is that you do not know Bosambo."

Hamilton was wakened at three in the next morning by the telegraph operator. It was a "clear the line" message, coded from headquarters, and half awake he went into Sanders' study and put it into plain English.

"Hope you are watching the Ochori border," it ran, "representations from French Government to the effect that a crossing is imminent."

He pulled his mosquito boots on over his pyjamas, struggled into a coat and crossed to Lieutenant Tibbetts' quarters.

Bones occupied a big hut at the end of the Houssa lines, and Hamilton woke him by the simple expedient of flashing his electric hand-lamp in his face.

B.—G

"I have had a telegram," he said, and Bones leapt out of bed wide awake in an instant.

"I knew jolly well I would draw a horse," he said exultantly. "I had a dream——"

"Be serious, you feather-minded devil."

With that Hamilton handed him the telgram.

Bones read it carefully, and interpreted any meanings into its construction which it could not possibly bear.

"What are you going to do?" he asked.

"There is only one thing to do," said Hamilton. "We shall have to take all the men we can possibly muster, and go north at daybreak."

"Spoken like a jolly old Hannibal," said Bones heartily, and smacked his superior on the back. A shrill bugle call aroused the sleeping lines, and Hamilton went back to his quarters to make preparations for the journey. In the first grey light of dawn he flew three pigeons to Bosambo, and the message they carried about their red legs was brief.

"Take your fighting regiments to the edge of Frenchi land; presently I will come with my soldiers and support you. Let no foreigner pass on your life and on your head."

When the rising sun tipped the tops of the palms with gold, and the wild world was filled with the sound of the birds, the *Zaire*, her decks alive with soldiers, began her long journey northward.

Just before the boat left, Hamilton received a further message from the Administrator. It was in plain English, some evidence of Sir Robert Sanleigh's haste.

"Confidential: This matter on the Ochori border extremely delicate. Complete adequate arrangements to keep in touch with me."

For one moment Hamilton conceived the idea of leaving Bones behind to deal with the telegram and come along. A little thought, however, convinced him of the futility of this method. For one thing he would want every bit of assistance he could get, and although Bones had his disadvantages he was an excellent soldier, and a loyal and gallant comrade.

It might be necessary for Hamilton to divide up his forces; in which case he could hardly dispense with Lieutenant Tibbetts, and he explained unnecessarily to Bones:

"I think you are much better under my eye where I can see what you're doing."

"Sir," said Bones very seriously, "it is not what I do, it is what I think. If you could only see my brain at work——"

"Ha, ha!" said Hamilton rudely.

For at least three days relations were strained between the two officers. Bones was a man who admitted at regular intervals that he was unduly sensitive. He had explained this disadvantage to Hamilton at various times, but the Houssa stolidly refused to remember the fact.

Most of the way up the river Hamilton attended to his business navigation—he knew the stream very well—whilst Bones, in a cabin which had been rigged up for him in the after part of the ship, played Patience, and by a systematic course of cheating himself was able to accomplish marvels. They found the Ochori city deserted save for a strong guard, for Bosambo had marched the day previous; sending a war call through the country.

He had started with a thousand spears, and his force was growing in snowball fashion as he progressed through the land. The great road which Notiki, the northern chief, had started by way of punishment was beginning to take shape. Bosambo had moved with incredible swiftness.

Too swift, indeed, for a certain Angolian-Congo robber who had headed a villainous pilgrimage to a land which, as he had predicted, flowed with milk and honey; was guarded by timorous men and mainly populated by slim and beautiful maidens. The Blue Books on this migration gave this man's name as Kisini, but he was in fact an Angolian named Bizaro

—a composite name which smacks suspiciously of Portuguese influence.

Many times had the unruly people and the lawless bands which occupied the forest beyond the Ochori threatened to cross into British territory. But the dangers of the unknown, the awful stories of a certain white lord who was swift to avenge and monstrously inquisitive had held them. Year after year there had grown up tribes within tribes, tiny armed camps that had only this in common, that they were outside the laws from which they had fled, and that somewhere to the southward and the eastward were strong forces flying the tricolour of France or the yellow star of the Belgian Congo, ready to belch fire at them, if they so much as showed their flat noses.

It would have needed a Napoleon to have combined all the conflicting forces, to have lulled all the mutual suspicions, and to have moulded these incompatible particles into a whole; but, Bizaro, like many another vain and ambitious man, had sought by means of a great palaver to produce a feeling of security sufficiently soothing to the nerves and susceptibilities of all elements, to create something like a nationality of these scattered remnants of the nations.

And though he failed, he did succeed in bringing together four or five of the camps, and it was this news carried to the French Governor by spies, transmitted to Downing Street, and flashed back to the Coast, which set Hamilton and his Houssas moving; which brought a regiment of the King's African Rifles to the Coast ready to reinforce the earlier expedition, and which (more to the point) had put Bosambo's war drums rumbling from one end of the Ochorito to the other.

Bizaro, mustering his force, came gaily through the sunsplashed aisles of the forest, his face streaked hideously with camwood, his big elephant spear twirled between his fingers, and behind him straggled his cosmopolitan force.

There were men from the Congo and the French Congo;

men from German lands; from Angola; wanderers from far-off Barotseland, who had drifted on to the Congo by the swift and yellow Kasai. There were hunters from the forests of far-off Bongindanga where the *okapi* roams. For each man's presence in that force there was good and sinister reason, for these were no mere tax-evaders, poor, starved wretches fleeing from the rule which *Bula Matadi*[1] imposed. There was a blood price on almost every head, and in a dozen prisons at Boma, at Brazaville, and Equatorville, and as far south as St. Paul de Loduda, there were leg-irons which had at some time or other fitted their scarred ankles.

Now there are four distinct physical features which mark the border line between the border land and the foreign territory. Mainly the line is a purely imaginary one, not traceable save by the most delicate instruments—a line which runs through a tangle of forest.

But the most noticeable crossing place is N'glili.[2]

Here a little river, easily fordable, and not more than a dozen spear-lengths across flows from one wood into another. Between the two woods is a clear space of thick grass and shrub. In the spring of the year the banks of the stream are white with arum-lilies, and the field beyond, at a later period, is red with wild anemone.

The dour fugitives on the other side of the stream have a legend that those who safely cross the "Field of Blood" —so they call the anemone-sprinkled land beyond—without so much as crushing a flower may claim sanctuary under the British flag.

So that when Bizaro sighted the stream, and the two tall trees that flanked the ford, from afar off and said: "Today we will walk between the flowers," he was signifying the definite character of his plans.

"Master," said one of the more timid of his muster, when

[1] The stone breaker, the native name for the Congo Government.
[2] Probably a corruption of the word "English."

they had halted for a rest in sight of the promised land, "what shall we do when we come to these strange places?"

"We shall defeat all manner of men," said Bizaro optimistically. "Afterwards they shall come and sue for peace, and they shall give us a wide land where we may build us huts and sow our corn. And they also will give us women, and we shall settle in comfort, and I will be chief over you. And, growing with the moons, in time I shall make you a great nation."

They might have crossed the stream that evening and committed themselves irrevocably to their invasion. Bizaro was a criminal, and a lazy man, and he decided to sleep where he was—an act fatal to the smooth performance of his enterprise, for when in the early hours of the morning he marched his horde to the N'glili river he found two thousand spears lining the opposite bank, and they were under a chief who was at once insolent and unmoved by argument.

"O chief," said Bosambo pleasantly, "you do not cross my beautiful flowers today."

"Lord," said Bizaro humbly, "we are poor men who desire a new land."

"That you shall have," said Bosambo grimly, "for I have sent my warriors to dig big holes wherein you may take your rest in this land you desire."

An unhappy Bizaro carried his six hundred spears slowly back to the land from whence he had come and found on return to the mixed tribes that he had unconsciously achieved a miracle. For the news of armed men by the N'glili river carried terror to these evil men—they found themselves between two enemies and chose the force which they feared least.

On the fourth day following his interview with Bosambo, Bizaro led five thousand desperate men to the ford and there was a sanguinary battle which lasted for the greater part of the morning and was repeated at sundown.

Hamilton brought his Houssas up in the nick of time, when one wing of Bosambo's force was being thrust back and when Bizaro's desperate adventurers had gained the Ochori bank. Hamilton came through the clearing, and formed his men rapidly.

Sword in hand, in advance of the glittering bayonets, Bones raced across the red field, and after one brief and glorious mêlée the invader was driven back, and a dropping fire from the left, as the Houssas shot steadily at the flying enemy, completed the disaster to Bizaro's force.

"That settles *that*!" said Hamilton.

He had pitched his camp on the scene of his exploit, the bivouac fires of the Houssas gleamed redly amongst the anemones.

"Did you see me in action?" asked Bones, a little self-consciously.

"No, I didn't notice anything particularly striking about the fight in your side of the world," said Hamilton.

"I suppose you did not see me bowl over a big Congo chap?" asked Bones, carelessly, as he opened a tin of preserved tongue. "Two at once I bowled over," he repeated.

"What do you expect me to do?" asked Hamilton unpleasantly. "Get up and cheer, or recommend you for the Victoria Cross or something?"

Bones carefully speared a section of tongue from the open tin before he replied.

"I had not thought about the Victoria Cross, to tell you the truth," he admitted, "but if you feel that you ought to recommend me for something or other for conspicuous courage in the face of the enemy, do not let your friendship stand in the way."

"I will not," said Hamilton.

There was a little pause, then without raising his eyes from the task in hand which was at that precise moment the covering of a biscuit with a large and generous layer of marmalade, Bones went on:

"I practically saved the life of one of Bosambo's headmen. He was on the ground and three fellows were jabbing at him. The moment they saw me they dropped their spears and fled."

"I expect it was your funny nose that did the trick," said Hamilton unimpressed.

"I stood there," Bones went on loftily ignoring the gratuitous insult, "waiting for anything that might turn up; exposed, dear old fellow, to every death-dealing missile, but calmly directing, if you will allow me to say so, the tide of battle. It was," he added modestly, "one of the bravest deeds I ever saw."

He waited, but Hamilton had his mouth full of tongue sandwich.

"If you mention me in despatches," Bones went on suggestively.

"Don't worry—I shan't," said Hamilton.

"But if you did," persisted Lieutenant Tibbetts, poising his sticky biscuit, "I can only say——"

"The marmalade is running down your sleeve," said Hamilton. "Shut up, Bones, like a good chap."

Bones sighed.

"The fact of it is, Hamilton," he was frank enough to say, "I have been serving so far without hope of reward and scornful of honour, but now I have reached the age and the position in life where I feel I am entitled to some slight recognition to solace my declining years."

"How long have you been in the army?" asked Hamilton, curiously.

"Eighteen months," replied Bones; "nineteen months next week, and it's a jolly long time, I can tell you, sir."

Leaving his dissatisfied subordinate, Hamilton made the round of the camp. The red field, as he called it, was in reality a low-lying meadow, which rose steeply to the bank of the river on the one side and more steeply—since it first sloped downward in that direction—to the Ochori forest, two miles away. He made this discovery with a little feeling of alarm. He knew something of native tactics, and though his scouts had reported that the enemy was effectually routed, and that the nearest body was five miles away, he put a strong advance picquet on the other side of the river, and threw a wide cordon of sentries about the camp. Especially he apportioned Abiboo, his own sergeant, the task of watching the little river which flowed swiftly between its orderly banks past the sunken camp. For two days Abiboo watched and found nothing to report.

Not so the spies who were keeping watch upon the moving remnants of Bizaro's army.

They came with the news that the main body had mysteriously disappeared. To add to Hamilton's anxiety he received a message by way of headquarters and the Ochori city from the Administrator.

"Be prepared at the first urgent message from myself to fall back on the Ochori city. German Government claim that whole of country for two miles north of river N'glili is their territory. Most delicate situation. International complications feared. Rely on your discretion, but move swiftly if you receive orders."

"Leave this to me," said Bones when Hamilton read the message out. "Did I ever tell you, sir, that I was intended for the diplomatic service——"

* * * * *

The truth about the Ochori border has never been thoroughly exposed. If you get into your mind the fact that the Imperialists of four nations were dreaming dreams of a trans-African railway which was to tap the resources of the interior, and if you remember that each patriotic dreamer conceived a different kind of railway according to his nationality and that they only agreed upon one point, namely, that the line must point contiguous with the Ochori border, you may understand dimly some reason for the frantic claim that that little belt of territory, two miles wide, was part of the domain of each and every one of the contestants.

When the news was flashed to Europe that a party of British Houssas were holding the banks of the N'glili river, and had inflicted a loss upon a force of criminals, the approval which civilisation should rightly have bestowed upon Captain Hamilton and his heroic lieutenant was tempered largely by the question as to whether Captain Hamilton and his Houssas had any right whatever to be upon "the red field." And in consequence the telegraph lines between Berlin and Paris and Paris and London and London and Brussels were kept fairly busy with passionate statements of claims couched in the stilted terminology of diplomacy.

England could not recede from the position she had taken. This she said in French and in German, and in her own perfidious tongue. She stated this uncompromisingly, but at the same time sent secret orders to withdraw the force that was the bone of contention. This order she soon countermanded. A certain speech delivered by a too voluble Belgian minister was responsible for the stiffening of her back, and His Excellency the Administrator of the territory received official instructions in the middle of the night: "Tell Hamilton to stay where he is and hold border against all comers."

This message was re-transmitted.

Now there is in existence in the British Colonial Service, and in all branches which affect the agents and the servants of the Colonial Office, an emergency code which is based upon certain characters in Shakespearean plays.

I say "there is"; perhaps it would be better and more to the point if I said "there was," since the code has been considerably amended.

Thus, be he sub-inspector or commissioner, or chief of local native police who receives the word "Ophelia," he knows without consulting any book that "Ophelia" means

"unrest of natives reported in your district, please report";
or if it be "Polonius" it signifies to him—and this he knows
without confirming his knowledge—that he must move
steadily forward. Or if it be "Banquo" he reads into it,
"Hold your position till further orders." And "Banquo"
was the word that the Administrator telegraphed.

* * * * *

Sergeant Abiboo had sat by the flowing N'glili river without noticing any slackening of its strength or challenging
of its depth.

There was reason for this.

Bizaro, who was in the forest ten miles to the westward,
and working, moreover, upon a piece of native strategy which
natives the world over had found successful, saw that it was
unnecessary to dam the river and divert the stream.

Nature had assisted him to a marvellous degree. He had
followed the stream through the forest until he reached a
place where it was a quarter of a mile wide, so wide and so
newly spread that the water reached half-way up the trunks
of the sodden and dying trees.

Moreover, there was a bank through which a hundred
men might cut a breach in a day or so, even though they went
about their work most leisurely, being constitutionally
averse to manual labour.

Bizaro was no engineer, but he had all the forest man's
instincts of water-levels. There was a clear run down to
the meadows beyond that, as he said, he "smelt."

"We will drown these dogs," he said to his headman,
"and afterwards we will walk into the country and take it
for our own."

Hamilton had been alive to the danger of such an attack.
He saw by certain indications of the soil that this great
shallow valley had been inundated more than once, though
probably many years had passed since the last overflow of

water. Yet he could not move from where he had planted himself without risking the displeasure of his chief and without also risking very serious consequences in other directions.

Bosambo, frankly bored, was all for retiring his men to the comforts of the Ochori city.

"Lord, why do we sit here?" he asked, "looking at this little stream which has no fish and at this great ugly country, when I have my beautiful city for your lordship's reception, and dancing folk and great feasts?"

"A doocid sensible idea," murmured Bones.

"I wait for a book," answered Hamilton shortly. "If you wish to go, you may take your soldiers and leave me."

"Lord," said Bosambo, "you put shame on me," and he looked his reproach.

"I am really surprised at you, Hamilton," murmured Bones.

"Keep your infernal comments to yourself," snapped his superior. "I tell you I must wait for my instructions."

He was a silent man for the rest of the evening, and had settled himself down in his canvas chair to doze away the night, when a travel-stained messenger came from the Ochori and he brought a telegram of one word.

Hamilton looked at it, he looked too with a frown at the figures that followed it.

"And what you mean," he muttered, "the Lord knows!"

The word, however, was sufficiently explicit. A bugle call brought the Houssas into line and the tapping of Bosambo's drums assembled his warriors.

Within half an hour of the receipt of the message Hamilton's force was on the move.

They crossed the great stretch of meadow in the darkness and were climbing up towards the forest when a noise like thunder broke upon their ears.

Such a roaring, crashing, hissing of sound came nearer and nearer, increasing in volume every second. The sky was clear, and one swift glance told Hamilton that it was not a storm he had to fear. And then it came upon him, and he realised what this commotion meant.

"Run!" he cried, and with one accord naked warriors and uniformed Houssas fled through the darkness to the higher ground. The water came rushing about Hamilton's ankles, one man slipped back again into the flood and was hauled out again by Bones, exclaiming loudly his own act lest it should have escaped the attention of his superior, and the party reached safety without the loss of a man.

"Just in time," said Hamilton grimly. "I wonder if the Administrator knew this was going to happen?"

They came to Ochori by easy marches, and Hamilton wrote a long wire to headquarters sending it on ahead by a swift messenger.

It was a dispatch which cleared away many difficulties, for the disputed territory was for everlasting under water, and where the "red field" had blazed brilliantly was a calm stretch of river two miles wide filled with strange silent brown objects that floated and bobbed to the movement of the tide. These were the men who in their folly had loosened the waters and died of their rashness. Most notable of these was Bizaro.

There was a shock waiting for Hamilton when he reached the Ochori city. The wire from the Administrator was kindly enough and sufficiently approving to satisfy even an exigent Bones. "But," it ran, "why did you retire in face of stringent orders to remain? I wired you 'Banquo.'"

Hamilton afterwards learnt that the messenger carrying this important dispatch had passed his party in their retirement through the forest.

"Banquo," quoted Hamilton in amazement. "I received absolute instructions to retire."

"Hard cheese," said Bones, sympathetically. "His dear old Excellency wants a good talking to; but are you sure, dear old chap, that you haven't made a mistake."

"Here it is," he said, "but I must confess that I don't understand the numbers."

He handed it to Bones. It read:

"Mercutio 17178."

Bones looked at it a moment, then gasped. He reached out his hand solemnly and grasped that of the astounded Hamilton.

"Dear old fellow," he said in a broken voice, "congratulate me, I have drawn a runner!"

"A runner?"

"A runner, dear old sport," chortled Bones, "in the Cambridgeshire! You see, I've got a ticket number seventeen, seventeen eight in my pocket, dear old friend! If Mercutio wins," he repeated solemnly, "I will stand you the finest dinner that can be secured this side of Romano's."

CHAPTER VI

THE SOUL OF THE NATIVE WOMAN

MAIL day is ever a day of supreme interest for the young and for the matter of that for the middle-aged, too. Sanders hated mail days because the bulk of his correspondence had to do with Government, and Government never sat down with a pen in its hand to wish Sanders many happy returns of the day or to tell him scandalous stories about mutual friends.

Rather the Government (by inference) told him scandalous stories about himself—of work not completed to the satisfaction of Downing Street—a thoroughfare given to expecting miracles.

Hamilton had a sister who wrote wittily and charmingly every week, and there was another girl. . . . Still, two letters and a bright pink paper or two made a modest postbag by the side of Lieutenant Tibbetts' mail.

There came to Bones every mail day a thick wad of letters and parcels innumerable, and he could sit at the big table for hours on end, whistling a little out of tune, mumbling incoherently. He had a trick of commenting upon his letters aloud, which was very disconcerting for Hamilton. Bones would open a letter and get half-way through it before he began his commenting.

"... poor soul ... dear! dear! ... what a silly old ass ... ah, would you ..... don't do it, Billy ..."

To Hamilton's eyes the bulk of correspondence rather increased than diminished.

"You must owe a lot of money," he said one day.

"Eh!"

"All these ...!" Hamilton opened his hand to a floor littered with discarded envelopes. "I suppose they represent demands ...."

"Dear lad," said Bones brightly, "they represent popularity—I'm immensely popular, sir," he gulped a little as he fished out two dainty envelopes from the pile before him; "you may not have experienced the sensation, but I assure you, sir, it's pleasing, it's doocidly pleasing!"

"Complacent ass," said Hamilton, and returned to his own correspondence.

Systematically Bones went through his letters, now and again consulting a neat little morocco-covered note-book. (It would appear he kept a very careful record of every letter he wrote home, its contents, the date of its despatch, and the reply thereto.) He had reduced letter writing to a passion, spent most of his evenings writing long epistles to his friends—mostly ladies of a tender age—and had incidentally acquired a reputation in the Old Country for his brilliant powers of narrative.

This, Hamilton discovered quite by accident. It would appear that Hamilton's sister had been on a visit—was in fact on the visit when she wrote one letter which so opened

Hamilton's eyes—and mentioned that she was staying with some great friends of Bones'. She did not, of course, call him "Bones," but "Mr. Tibbette."

"I should awfully like to meet him," she wrote, "he must be a very interesting man. Aggie Vernon had a letter from him yesterday wherein he described his awful experience lion-hunting.

"To be chased by a lion and caught and then carried to the beast's lair must have been awful!

"Mr. Tibbetts is very modest about it in his letter, and beyond telling Aggie that he escaped by sticking his finger in the lion's eye he says little of his subsequent adventure. By the way, Pat, Aggie tells me that you had a bad bout of fever and that Mr. Tibbetts carried you for some miles to the nearest doctor. I wish you wouldn't keep these things so secret, it worries me dreadfully unless you tell me—even the worst about yourself. I hope your interesting friend returned safely from his dangerous expedition into the interior—he was on the point of leaving when his letter was despatched and was quite gloomy about his prospects. . . ."

Hamilton read this epistle over and over again, then he sent for Bones.

That gentleman came most cheerfully, full of fine animal spirits, and——

"Just had a letter about you, Bones," said Hamilton carelessly.

"About me, sir!" said Bones, "from the War Office—I'm not being decorated or anything!" he asked anxiously.

"No—nothing so tragic; it was a letter from my sister, who is staying with the Vernons."

"Oh!" said Bones going suddenly red.

"What a modest devil you are," said the admiring Hamilton, "having a lion hunt all to yourself and not saying a word about it to anybody."

Bones made curious apologetic noises.

"I didn't know there were any lions in the country," pursued Hamilton remorselessly. "Liars, yes! But lions, no! I suppose you brought them with you—and I suppose, you know also, Bones, that it is considered in lion-hunting circles awfully rude to stick your finger into a lion's eye? It is bad sportsmanship to say the least, and frightfully painful for the lion."

Bones was making distressful grimaces.

"How would you like a lion to stick his finger in *your* eye?" asked Hamilton severely; "and, by the way, Bones, I have to thank you."

He rose solemnly, took the hand of his reluctant and embarrassed second and wrung.

"Thank you," said Hamilton, in a broken voice, "for saving my life."

"Oh, I say, sir," began Bones feebly.

"To carry a man eighty miles on your back is no mean accomplishment, Bones—especially when I was unconscious——"

"I didn't say you were unconscious, sir. In fact, sir——" floundered Lieutenant Tibbetts as red as a peony.

"And yet I was unconscious," insisted Hamilton firmly. "I am still unconscious, even to this day. I have no recollection of your heroic effort; Bones, I thank you."

"Well, sir," said Bones, "to make a clean breast of the whole affair——"

"And this dangerous expedition of yours, Bones, an expedition from which you might never return—that," said Hamilton in a hushed voice, "is the best story I have heard for years."

"Sir," said Bones, speaking under the stress of considerable emotion, "I am clean bowled, sir. The light-hearted fairy stories which I write to cheer, so to speak, the sick-bed of an innocent child, sir, they have recoiled upon my own head. *Peccavi, mea culpi,* an' all those jolly old expressions that you'll find in the back pages of the dictionary."

"Oh, Bones, Bones!" chuckled Hamilton.

"You mustn't think I'm a perfect liar, sir," began Bones, earnestly.

"I don't think you're a perfect liar," answered Hamilton, "I think you're the most inefficient liar I've ever met."

"Not even a liar, I'm a romancist, sir," Bones stiffened with dignity and saluted, but whether he was saluting Hamilton, or the spirit of Romance, or in sheer admiration was saluting himself, Hamilton did not know.

"The fact is, sir," said Bones confidentially, "I'm writing a book!"

He stepped back as though to better observe the effect of his words.

"What about?" asked Hamilton, curiously.

"About things I've seen and things I know," said Bones, in his most impressive manner.

"Oh, I see!" said Hamilton. "One of those waistcoat-pocket books."

Bones swallowed the insult with a gulp.

"I've been asked to write a book," he said, "my adventures an' all that sort of thing. Of course they needn't have happened, really——"

"In that case, Bones, I'm with you," said Hamilton. "If you're going to write a book about things that haven't happened to you, there's no limit to its size."

"You're bein' a jolly cruel old officer, sir," said Bones, pained by the cold cynicism of his chief. "But I'm very serious, sir. This country is full of material. And everybody says I ought to write a book about it—why, dash it, sir, I've been here nearly two months!"

"It seems years," said Hamilton.

Bones was perfectly serious, as he had said. He did intend preparing a book for publication, had dreams of a great literary career, and an ultimate membership of the Athenæum Club belike. It had come upon him like a revelation that such a career called him. The week after he had definitely made up his mind to utilise his gifts in this direction, his outgoing mail was heavier than ever. For to three and twenty English and American publishers, whose names he culled from a handy work of reference, he advanced a business-like offer to prepare for the press a volume "of 316 pages printed in type about the same size as enclosed," and to be entitled:

MY WILD LIFE AMONGST CANNIBALS
BY
Augustus Tibbetts, Lieutenant of Houssas
Fellow of the Royal Geographical Society; Fellow of the Royal Asiatic Society; Member of the Ethnological Society and Junior Army Service Club.

Bones had none of these qualifications, save the latter, but as he told himself he'd jolly soon be made a member if his book was a howling success.

No sooner had his letters been posted than he changed his mind, and he addressed three and twenty more letters to the publishers, altering the title to:

THE TYRANNY OF THE WILDS
Being Some Observations on the Habits and Customs of Savage Peoples
BY
Augustus Tibbetts (Lt.)
With a Foreword by Captain Patrick Hamilton.

"You wouldn't mind writing a foreword, dear old fellow?" he asked.

"Charmed," said Hamilton. "Have you a particular preference for any form?"

"Just please yourself, sir," said a delighted Bones, so Hamilton covered two sheets of foolscap with an appreciation which began:

"The audacity of the author of this singularly uninformed work is to be admired without necessarily being imitated. Two months' residence in a land which offered many opportunities for acquiring inaccurate data, has resulted in a work which must stand for all time as a monument of murderous effort," etc.

Bones read the appreciation very carefully.

"Dear old sport," he said, a little troubled, as he reached the end, "this is almost uncomplimentary."

You couldn't depress Bones or turn him from his set purpose. He scribed away, occupying his leisure moments with his great work. His normal correspondence suffered cruelly, but Bones was relentless. Hamilton sent him north to collect the hut tax, and at first Bones resented this order, believing that it was specially designed to hamper him.

"Of course, sir," he said, "I'll obey you, if you order me in accordance with regulations an' all that sort of rot, but believe me, sir, you're doin' an injury to literature. Unborn generations, sir, will demand an explanation——"

"Get out!" said Hamilton crossly.

Bones found his trip a blessing that had been well disguised. There were many points of interest on which he required first-hand information. He carried with him to the *Zaire* large exercise books on which he had pasted such pregnant labels as "Native Customs," "Dances," "Ju-jus," "Ancient Legends," "Folk-lore," etc. They were mostly blank, and represented projected chapters of his great work.

All might have been well with Bones. More virgin pages might easily have been covered with his sprawling writing and the book itself, converted into honest print, have found its way, in the course of time, into the tuppenny boxes of the Farringdon book-mart, sharing its soiled magnificence with the work of the best of us, but on his way Bones had a brilliant inspiration. There was a chapter he had not thought of, a chapter heading which had not been born to his mind until that flashing moment of genius.

Upon yet another exercise book, he pasted the label of a chapter which was to eclipse all others in interest. Behold then, this enticing announcement, boldly printed and ruled about with double lines:

"THE SOUL OF THE NATIVE WOMAN."

It was a fine chapter title. It was sonorous, it had dignity, it was full of possibilities. "The Soul of the Native Woman," repeated Bones, in an ecstasy of self-admiration, and having chosen his subject he proceeded to find out something about it.

Now, about this time, Bosambo of the Ochori might, had he wished and had he the literary quality, have written many books about women, if for no other reason than because of a certain girl named D'riti.

She was a woman of fifteen, grown to a splendid figure, with a proud head and a chin that tilted in contempt, for she was the daughter of Bosambo's chief counsellor, granddaughter of an Ochori king, and ambitious to be wife of Bosambo himself.

"This is a mad thing," said Bosambo when her father offered the suggestion, "for, as you know, T'meli, I have one wife who is a thousand wives to me."

"Lord, I will be ten thousand," said D'riti, present at the interview and bold; "also, Lord, it was predicted at my birth that I should marry a king and the greater than a king."

"That is me," said Bosambo, who was without modesty, "yet, it cannot be."

So they married D'riti to a chief's son who beat her till one day she broke his thick head with an iron pot, whereupon he sent her back to her father demanding the return of his dowry and the value of his pot.

She had her following, for she was a dancer of fame and could twist her lithe body into enticing shapes. She might have married again, but she was so scornful of common men that none dare ask for her. Also the incident of the iron pot was not forgotten, and D'riti went swaying through the village—she walked from the hips, gracefully—a straight, brown, girl-woman desired and unasked.

For she knew men too well to inspire confidence in them. By some weird intuition which certain women of all races acquire, she had probed behind their minds and saw with their eyes, and when she spoke of men, she spoke with a conscious authority, and such men, who were within earshot of her vitriolic comments, squirmed uncomfortably, and called her a woman of shame.

So matters stood when the *Zaire* came flashing to the Ochori city and the heart of Bones filled with pleasant anticipation.

Who was so competent to inform him on the matter of the souls of native women as Bosambo of the Ochori, already a crony of Bones, and admirable, if for no other reason, because he professed an open reverence for his new master? At any rate, after the haggle of tax collection was finished, Bones set about his task.

"Bosambo," said he, "men say you are very wise. Now tell me something about the women of the Ochori."

Bosambo looked at Bones a little startled.

"Lord," said he, "who knows about women? For is it not written in the blessed Sura of the Djin that women and death are beyond understanding?"

"That may be true," said Bones, "yet, behold, I make a book full of wise and wonderful things and it would be neither wise nor wonderful if there was no word of women."

And he explained very seriously indeed that he desired to know of the soul of native womanhood, of her thoughts and her dreams and her high desires.

"Lord," said Bosambo, after a long thought, "go to your

118

ship: presently I will send to you a girl who thinks and speaks with great wisdom—and if she talks with you, you shall learn more things than I can tell you."

To the *Zaire* at sundown came D'riti, a girl of proper height, hollow backed, bare to the waist, with a thin skirting of fine silk cloth which her father had brought from the Coast, wound tightly about her, yet not so tightly that it hampered her swaying, lazy walk. She stood before a disconcerted Bones, one small hand resting on her hip, her chin (as usual) tilted down at him from under lashes uncommonly long for a native.

Also, this Bones saw, she was gifted with more delicate features than the native woman can boast as a rule. The nose was straight and narrow, the lips full, yet not of the negroid type. She was in fact a pure Ochori woman, and the Ochori are related dimly to the Arabi tribes.

"Lord, Bosambo the King has sent me to speak about women," she said simply.

"Doocidly awkward," said Bones to himself, and blushed.

"O, D'riti," he stammered, "it is true I wish to speak of women, for I make a book that all white lords will read."

"Therefore have I come," she said. "Now listen, O my lord, whilst I tell you of women, and of all they think, of their love for men and of the strange way they show it. Also of children——"

"Look here," said Bones, loudly. "I don't want any—any—private information, my child——"

Then realising from her frown that she did not understand him, he returned to Bomongo.

"Lord, I will say what is to be said," she remarked, meekly, "for you have a gentle face and I see that your heart is very pure."

Then she began, and Bones listened with open mouth . . . later he was to feel his hair rise and was to utter gurgling protests, for she spoke with primitive simplicity about things that are never spoken about at all. He tried to check her, but she was not to be checked.

"Goodness, gracious heavens!" gasped Bones.

She told him of what women think of men, and of what men *think* women think of them, and there was a remarkable discrepancy if she spoke the truth. He asked her if she was married.

"Lord," she said at last, eyeing him thoughtfully, "it is written that I shall marry one who is greater than chiefs."

"I'll bet you will, too," thought Bones, sweating.

At parting she took his hand and pressed it to her cheek.

"Lord," she said softly, "tomorrow when the sun is nearly down, I will come again and tell you more . . ."

Bones left before daybreak, having all the material he wanted for his book and more.

He took his time descending the river, calling at sundry places.

At Ikan he tied up the *Zaire* for the night, and whilst his men were carrying the wood aboard, he settled himself to put down the gist of his discoveries. In the midst of his labours came Abiboo.

"Lord," said he, "there has just come by a fast canoe the woman who spoke with you last night."

"Jumping Moses!" said Bones, turning pale, "say to this woman that I am gone——"

But the woman came round the corner of the deck-house, shyly, yet with a certain confidence.

"Lord," she said, "behold I am here, your poor slave; there are wonderful things about women which I have not told you——"

"O, D'riti!" said Bones in despair, "I know all things, and it is not lawful that you should follow me so far from your home lest evil be said of you."

He sent her to the hut of the chief's wife—M'lini-fo-bini of Ikan—with instructions that she was to be returned to her home on the following morning. Then he went back to his work, but found it strangely distasteful. He left nothing to chance the next day.

With the dawn he slipped down the river at full speed, never so much as halting till day began to fail, and he was a short day's journey from headquarters.

"Anyhow, the poor dear won't overtake me today," he said—only to find the "poor dear" had stowed herself away on the steamer in the night behind a pile of wood.

*　　*　　*　　*　　*

"It's very awkward," said Hamilton, and coughed.

Bones looked at his chief pathetically.

"It's doocid awkward, sir?" he agreed dismally.

"You say she won't go back?"

Bones shook his head.

"She said I'm the moon and the sun an' all sorts of rotten things to her, sir," he groaned and wiped his forehead.

"Send her to me," said Hamilton.

"Be kind to her, sir," pleaded the miserable Bones. "After all, sir, the poor girl seems to be fond of me, sir—the human heart, sir—I don't know why she should take a fancy to me."

"That's what I want to know," said Hamilton, briefly, "if she *is* mad, I'll send her to the mission hospital along the Coast."

"You've a hard and bitter heart," said Bones, sadly.

D'riti came ready to flash her anger and eloquence at Hamilton; on the verge of defiance.

"D'riti," said Hamilton, "tomorrow I send you back to your people."

"Lord, I stay with Tibbetti who loves women and is happy to talk of them. Also some day I shall be his wife, for this is foretold." She shot a tender glance at poor Bones.

"That cannot be," said Hamilton calmly, "for Tibbetti has three wives, and they are old and fierce——"

"Oh, lord!" wailed Bones.

"And they would beat you and make you carry wood and water," Hamilton said; he saw the look of apprehension steal into the girl's face. "And more than this, D'riti, the Lord Tibbetti is mad when the moon is in full, he foams at the mouth and bites, uttering awful noises."

"Oh, dirty trick!" almost sobbed Bones.

"Go, therefore, D'riti," said Hamilton, "and I will give you a piece of fine cloth, and beads of many colours."

It is a matter of history that D'riti went.

"I don't know what you think of me, sir," said Bones, humbly, "of course I couldn't get rid of her——"

"You didn't try," said Hamilton, searching his pockets for his pipe. "You could have made her drop you like a shot."

"How, sir,?"

"Stuck your finger in her eye," said Hamilton, and Bones swallowed hard.

CHAPTER VII

THE STRANGER WHO WALKED BY NIGHT

SINCE the day when Lieutenant Francis Augustus Tibbetts rescued from the sacrificial trees the small brown baby whom he afterwards christened Henry Hamilton Bones, the interests of that young officer were to a very large extent extremely concentrated upon that absorbing problem which a famous journal once popularised, "What shall we do with our boys?"

As to the exact nature of the communications which Bones made to England upon the subject, what hairbreadth escapes and desperate adventure he detailed with that facile pen of his, who shall say?

It is unfortunate that Hamilton's sister—that innocent

purveyor of home news—had no glimpse of the correspondence, and that other recipients of his confidence are not in touch with the writer of these chronicles. Whatever he wrote, with what fervour he described his wanderings in the forest no one knows, but certainly he wrote to some purpose.

"What the dickens are all these parcels that have come for you for?" demanded his superior officer, eyeing with disfavour a mountain of brown paper packages be-sealed, bestringed, and be-stamped.

Bones, smoking his pipe, turned them over.

"I don't know for certain," he said, carefully; "but I shouldn't be surprised if they aren't clothes, dear old officer."

"Clothes?"

"For Henry," explained Bones, and cutting the string of one and tearing away its covering revealed a little mountain of snowy garments. Bones turned them over one by one.

"For Henry," he repeated. "Could you tell me, sir, what these things are for?"

He held up a garment white and small and frilly.

"No, sir, I can't," said Hamilton stiffly, "unless like the ass that you are you have forgotten to mention to your friends that Henry is a gentleman child."

Bones looked up at the blue sky and scratched his chin.

"I may have called him 'her'," he confessed.

There were, to be exact, sixteen parcels and each contained at least one such garment, and in addition a very warm shawl, "which," said Hamilton, "will be immensely useful when it snows."

With the aid of his orderly, Bones sorted out the wardrobe and the playthings (including many volumes of the Oh-look-at-the-rat-on-the-mat-where-is-the-cat? variety), and these he carried to his hut with such dignity as he could summon.

That evening, Hamilton paid his subordinate a visit. Henry, pleasingly arrayed in a pair of the misdirected garments with a large bonnet on his head, and seated on the floor of the quarters contentedly chewing Bones' watch, the whilst Bones, accompanying himself with his banjo, was singing a song which was chiefly remarkable for the fact that he was ignorant of the tune and somewhat hazy concerning the words.

> "Did you ever take a tum-ty up the Nile,
> Did you ever dumty dumty in a camp,
> Or dumpty dumpty on m—m——
> Or play it in a dumty dumty swamp."

He rose, and saluted his senior, as Hamilton came in.

"Exactly what is going to happen when Sanders comes back?" asked Hamilton, and the face of Bones fell.

"Happen, sir? I don't take you, sir—what *could* happen —to whom, sir?"

"To Henry," said Hamilton.

Henry looked up at that moment with a seraphic smile.

"Isn't he wonderful, sir?" asked Bones in hushed ecstasy. "You won't believe what I'm going to tell you, sir—you're such a jolly old sceptic, sir—but Henry knows me—positively recognises me! And when you remember that he's only four months old—why, it's unbelievable."

"But what will you do when Sanders comes—really, Bones, I don't know whether I ought to allow this as it is."

"If exception is taken to Henry, sir," said Bones firmly, "I resign my commission; if a gentleman is allowed to keep a dog, sir, he is surely allowed to keep a baby. Between Henry and me, sir, there is a bond stronger than steel. I may be an ass, sir, I may even be a goop, but come between me an' my child an' all my motherly instincts—if you'll pardon the paradox—all my paternal—that's the word— instincts are aroused, and I will fight like a tiger, sir——"

"What a devil you are for jaw," said Hamilton; "anyway, I've warned you. Sanders is due in a month."

124

"Henry will be five," murmured Bones.

"Oh, blow Henry!" said Hamilton.

Bones rose and pointed to the door.

"May I ask you, sir," he said, "not to use that language before the child? I hate to speak to you like this, sir, but I have a responsible——"

He dodged out of the open door and the loaf of bread which Hamilton had thrown struck the lintel and rolled back to Henry's eager hands.

The two men walked up and down the parade ground whilst Fa'ma, the wife of Ahmet, carried the child to her quarters where he slept.

"I'm afraid I've got to separate you from your child," said Hamilton; "there is some curious business going on in the Lombobo, and a stranger who walks by night, of which Ahmet the Spy writes somewhat confusingly."

Bones glanced round in some apprehension.

"Oblige me, old friend," he entreated, "by never speakin' of such things before Henry—I wouldn't have him scared for the world."

II

Bosambo of the Ochori was a light sleeper, the lighter because of certain stories which had reached him of a stranger who walks by night, and in the middle of the night he suddenly became wide awake, conscious that there was a man in his hut of whose coming the sentry without was ignorant.

Bosambo's hand went out stealthily for his short spear, but before he could reach it, his wrist was caught in a grip of steel, strong fingers gripped his throat, and the intruder whispered fiercely, using certain words which left the chief helpless with wonder.

"I am M'gani of the Night," said the voice with authoritative hauteur, "of me you have heard, for I am known only to chiefs; and am so high that chiefs obey and even devils go quickly from my path."

"O, M'gani, I hear you," whispered Bosambo, "how may I serve you?"

"Get me food," said the imperious stranger, "after, you shall make a bed for me in your inner room, and sit before this house that none may disturb me, for it is to my high purpose that no word shall go to M'ilitani that I stay in your territory."

"M'gani, I am your dog," said Bosambo, and stole forth from the hut like a thief to obey.

All that day he sat before his hut and even sent away the wife of his heart and the child M'sambo, that the rest of M'gani or the N'gombi should not be disturbed.

That night when darkness had come and the glowing red of hut fires grew dimmer, M'gani came from the hut.

Bosambo had sent away the guard and accompanied his guest to the end of the village.

M'gani, with only a cloak of leopard skin about him, twirling two long spears as he walked, was silent till he came to the edge of the city where he was to take farewell of his host.

"Tell me this, Bosambo, where are Sandi's spies that I may avoid them?"

And Bosambo, without hesitation, told him.

"M'gani," said he, at parting, "where do you go now? tell me that I may send cunning men to guard you, for there is a bad spirit in this land, especially amongst the people of Lombobo, because I have offended B'limi Saka, the chief."

"No soldiers do I need, O Bosambo," said the other. "Yet I tell you this that I go to quiet places to learn that which will be best for my people."

He turned to go.

"M'gani," said Bosambo, "in the day when you shall see our Lord Sandi, speak to him for me saying that I am faithful, for it seems to me, so high a man are you that he will listen to your word when he will listen to none other."

"I hear," said M'gani gravely, and slipped into the shadows of the forest.

Bosambo stood for a long time staring in the direction which M'gani had taken, then walked slowly back to his hut.

In the morning came the chief of his counsellors for a hut palaver.

"Bosambo," said he, in a tone of mystery, "the Walker-of-the-Night has been with us."

"Who says this?" asked Bosambo.

"Fibini, the fisherman," said the councillor, "for this he says, that having toothache, he sat in the shadow of his hut near the warm fire and saw the Walker pass through the village and with him, lord, one who was like a devil, being big and very ugly."

"Go to Fibini," said a justly annoyed Bosambo, "and beat him on the feet till he cries—for he is a liar and a spreader of alarm."

Yet Fibini had done his worst before the bastinado (an innovation of Bosambo's) had performed its silencing mission, and Ochori mothers shepherded their little flocks with greater care when the sun went down that night, for thio new terror which had come to the land, this black ghost with the wildfire fame was reputed especially devilish. In a week he had become famous—so swift does news carry in the territories.

Men had seen him passing through forest paths, or speeding with incredible swiftness along the silent river. Some said that he had no boat and walked the waters, others that he flew like a bat with millions of bats behind him. One had met him face to face and had sunk to the ground before eyes "that were very hot and red and thrusting out little lightnings."

He had been seen in many places in the Ochori, in the

N'gombi city, in the villages of the Akasava, but mainly his hunting ground was the narrow strip of territory which is called Lombobo.

B'limi Saka, the chief of the land, himself a believer in devils, was especially perturbed lest the Silent Walker should be a spy of Government, for he had been guilty of practices which were particularly obnoxious to the white men who were so swift to punish.

"Yet," said he to his daughter and (to the disgust of his people, who despised women) his chief councillor, "none know my heart save you, Lamalana."

Lamalana, with her man shoulders and her flat face, peered at her grizzled father sideways.

"Devils hear hearts," she said huskily, "and when they talk of killings and sacrifices are not all devils pleased? Now I tell you this, my father, that I wait for sacrifices which you swore by death you would show me."

B'limi Saka looked round fearfully. Though the ferocity of this chief was afterwards revealed, though secret places in the forest held his horrible secret killing-houses, yet he was a timid man with a certain affection of his eyes which made him dependent upon the childless widow who had been his strength for two years.

The Lombobo were the cruellest of Sanders' people; their chiefs the most treacherous. Neither akin to the N'gombi, the Isisi, the Akasava nor the Ochori, they took on the worst attributes of each race.

Seldom in open warfare did they challenge the Administration, but there was a long tale of slain and mutilated enemies who floated face downwards in the stream; of disappearance of faithful servants of Government, and of acts of cannibalism which went unidentified and unpunished.

For though all the tribes, save the Ochori, had been cannibals, yet by fire and rope, tempered with wisdom, had the Administration brought about a newer era to the upper river.

But reformation came not to the Lombobo. A word from Sanders, a carelessly expressed view, and the Lombobo people would have been swept from existence—wiped ruthlessly from the list of nations, but that was not the way of Government, which is patient and patient and patient again till in the end, by sheer heavy weight of patience, it crushes opposition to its wishes.

They called Lamalana the barren woman, the Drinker of Life, but she had at least drunken without ostentation, and if she murdered with her own large hands, or staked men and women from a sheer lust of cruelty, there were none alive to speak against her.

Outside the town of Lombobo[1] was a patch of beaten ground where no grass grew, and this place was called "wa boma," the killing ground.

Here, before the white men came, sacrifices were made openly, and it was perhaps for this association and because it was, from its very openness, free from the danger of the eavesdropper, that Lamalana and her father would sit by the hour, whilst he told her the story of ancient horrors— never too horrible for the woman who swayed to and fro as she listened as one who was hypnotised.

"Lord," said she, "the Walker of the Night comes not alone to the Lombobo; all my people up and down the river have seen him, and to my mind he is a sign of great fortune showing that ghosts are with us. Now, if you are very brave, we will have a killing greater than any. Is there no hole in the hill[2] which Bosambo dug for your shame? And, lord, do not the people of the Ochori say that this child M'sambo is the light of his father's life? O ko! Bosambo shall be sorry."

Later they walked in the forest speaking, for they had

---

[1] The territories are invariably named after the principal city, which is sometimes, perhaps, a little misleading.—E.W.

[2] See *A Right of Way* (chapter viii).

no fear of the spirits which the last slanting rays of the dying sun unlocked from the trees. And they talked and walked, and Lombobo huntsmen, returning through the wood, gave them a wide berth, for Lamalana was possessed of an eye which was notoriously evil.

"Let us go back to the city," said Lamalana, "for now I see that you are very brave and not a blind old man."

"There will be a great palaver and who knows but M'ilitani will come with his soldiers?"

She laughed loudly and hoarsely, making the silent forest ring with harsh noise.

"O ko!" she said, then laughed no more.

In the centre of the path was a man; in the half light she saw the leopard skin and the strange belt of metal about his waist.

"O Lamalana," he said softly, "laugh gently, for I have quick ears and I smell blood."

He pointed to the darkening forest path down which they had come.

"Many have been sacrificed and none heard them," he said, "this I know now. Let there be an end to killing, for I am M'gani, the Walker of the Night, and very terrible."

"Wa!" screamed Lamalana, and leapt at him with clawing hands and her white teeth agrin. Then something soft and damp struck her face—full in the mouth like a spray of water, and she fell over struggling for her breath, and rose gasping to her feet to find the Walker had gone.

III

Before Bosambo's hut Bones sat in a long and earnest conversation, and the subject of his discourse was children. For, alarmed by the ominous suggestion which Bones had put forward, that his superior should be responsible for the well-being of Henry in the absence of his foster-parent,

Hamilton had yielded to the request that Henry should accompany Bones on his visit to the north.

And now, on a large rug before Bosambo and his lord, there sat two small children eyeing one another with mutual distrust.

"Lord," said Bosambo, "it is true that your lordship's child is wonderful, but I think that M'sambo is also wonderful. If your lordship will look with kind eyes he will see a certain cunning way which is strange in so young a one. Also he speaks clearly so that I understand him."

"Yet," contested Bones, "as it seems to me, Bosambo, mine is very wise, for see how he looks to me when I speak, raising his thumb."

Bones made a clucking noise with his mouth, and Henry turned frowningly, regarded his protector with cool indifference, and returned to his scrutiny of the other strange brown animal confronting him.

"Now," said Bones that night, "what of the Walker?"

"Lord, I know of him," said Bosambo, "yet I cannot speak for we are blood brothers by certain magic rites and speeches; this I know, that he is a good man as I shall testify to Sandi when he comes back to his own people."

"You sit here for Government," said Bones, "and if you don't play the game you're a jolly old rotter, Bosambo!"

"I know 'um, I no speak 'um, sah," said Bosambo, "I be good fellah, sah, no Yadasi fellah, sah—I be Peter fellah, cut 'em ear some like, sah!"

"You're a naughty old humbug," said Bones, and went to bed on the *Zaire* leaving Henry with the chief's wife . . .

In the dark hours before the dawn he led his Houssas across the beach, revolver in hand, but came a little too late. The surprise party had been well planned. A speared sentry lay twisting before the chief's hut, and Bosambo's face was smothered in blood. Bones took in the situation.

"Fire on the men who fly to the forest," he said, but Bosambo laid a shaking hand upon his arm.

"Lord," he said, "hold your fire, for they have taken the children, and I fear the woman my wife is stricken."

He went into the hut, Bones following.

The chief's wife had a larger hut than Bosambo's own, communicating with her lord's through a passage of wicker and clay, and the raiders had clubbed her to silence, but Bones knew enough of surgery to see that she was in no danger.

In ten minutes the fighting regiments of the Ochori were sweeping through the forest, trackers going ahead to pick up the trail.

"Let all gods hear me," sobbed Bosambo, as he ran, "and send M'gani swiftly to M'sambo my son."

IV

"Now this is very wonderful," said Lamalana, "and it seems, O my father, no matter for a small killing, but for a sacrifice such as all men may see."

It was the hour following the dawn when the world was at its sweetest, when the chattering weaver birds went in and out of their hanging nests gossiping loudly, and faint perfumes from little morning flowers gave the air an unusual delicacy.

All the Lombobo people, the warriors and the hunters, the wives and the maidens, and even the children of tender years, lined the steep slopes of the Cup of Sacrifice. For Lamalana, deaf and blind to reason, knew that her hour was short, and that with the sun would come a man terrible in his anger . . . and the soldiers who eat up opposition with fire.

"O people!" she cried.

She was stripped to the waist, stood behind the Stone of Death as though it were a counter, and the two squirming infants under her hands were so much saleable stock:

"Here we bring terror to all who hate us, for one of these is the heart of Bosambo and the other is more than the heart of the man-who-stands-for-Sandi——"

"O woman!"

The intruder had passed unnoticed, almost it seemed by magic, through the throng, and now he stood in the clear space of sacrifice. And there was not one in the throng who had not heard of him with his leopard skin and his belt of brass.

He was as black as the strange Ethiopians who came sometimes to the land with the Arabo traders, his muscular arms and legs were dull in their blackness.

There was a whisper of terror—"The Walker of the Night!"—and the people fell back . . . a woman screamed and fell into a fit.

"O woman," said M'gani, "deliver to me these little children who have done no evil."

Open-mouthed the half-demented daughter of B'limi Saka stared at him.

He walked forward, lifted the children in his two arms and went slowly through the people, who parted in terror at his coming.

He turned at the top of the basin to speak.

"Do no wickedness," said he; then he gently stooped to put the two children on the ground, for mouthing and bellowing senseless sounds Lamalana came furiously after him, her long, crooked knife in her hand. He thrust his hand into the leopard skin as for a weapon, but before he could withdraw it, a man of Lombobo, half in terror, fell upon and threw his arms about M'gani.

"Bo'ma!" boomed the woman, and drew back her knife for the stroke. . . .

Bones, from the edge of the clearing, jerked up the rifle he carried and fired.

*   *   *   *   *

"What man is this?" asked Bones.

Bosambo looked at the stranger.

"This is M'gani," he said, "he who walks in the night."

"The dooce it is!" said Bones, and fixing his monocle glared at the stranger.

"From whence do you come?" he asked.

"Lord, I come from the Coast," said the man, "by many strange ways, desiring to arrive at this land secretly that I might learn the heart of these people and understand." Then, in perfect English, "I don't think we've ever met before, Mr. Tibbetts—my name is Sanders."

CHAPTER VIII

A RIGHT OF WAY

THE Borders of Territories may be fixed by treaty, by certain mathematical calculations, or by arbitrary proclamation. In the territories over which Sanders ruled they were governed as between tribe and tribe by custom and such natural lines of demarcation as a river or a creek supplied.

In forest land this was not possible, and there had ever been between the Ochori and the Lombobo a feud and a grievance, touched-up border fights, for hereabouts there is good hunting. Sanders had tried many methods and had hit upon the red gum border as a solution to a great difficulty. For some curious reason there were no red gum trees in the northern fringe of the forest for five miles on the Ochori side of the great wood; it was innocent of this beautiful tree and Sanders' fiat had gone forth that there should be no Ochori hunting in the red gum lands, and that settled the matter, and Sanders hoped for good.

But Bosambo set himself to enlarge his borders by a single expedient. Whenever his hunters came upon a red gum tree they cut it down. B'limi Saka, the chief of the sullen Lombobo, retaliated by planting red gum saplings on the country between the forest and the river—a fact of which Bosambo was not aware until he suddenly discovered a huge wedge of red gum driven into his lawful territory. A wedge so definite as to cut off nearly a thousand square miles of his territory, for beyond this border lay the lower Ochori country.

"How may I reach my proper villages?" he asked Sanders, who had known something of the comedy which was being enacted.

"You shall have canoes at the place of the young gum trees and shall row to a place beyond them," Sanders had said. "I have given my word that the red gum lands are the territory of B'limisaka, and since you have only your cunning to thank—Oh, cutter of trees—I cannot help you!"

Bosambo would have made short work of the young saplings, but B'limisaka established a guard not to be forced without bloodshed, and Bosambo could do no more in that way of reprisal than instruct his people to hurl insulting references to B'limisaka's as they passed the forbidden ground.

For the maddening thing was that the slip of filched territory was less than a hundred yards wide and men of the Lombobo, who went out by night to widen it, never came out alive—for Bosambo also had a guard.

Sometimes the minion spies of Government would come to headquarters with a twist of rice paper stuck in a quill, the quill inserted in the lobes of the ear in very much the same place as the ladies wore their earrings in the barbarous mid-Victorian period, and on the rice-paper with the briefest introduction would be inserted, in perfect Arabic, scraps of domestic news for the information of the Government.

Sometimes news would carry from mouth to mouth and a weary man would squat before Hamilton and recite his lesson.

"Efobi of the Isisi has stolen goats, and because he is the brother of the chief's wife goes unpunished; T'mara of the Akasava has put a curse upon the wife of O'femo the headman, and she has burnt his hut; N'kema of the Ochori will not pay his tax, saying that he is no Ochori man, but a true N'gombi; Bosambo's men have beaten a woodman of B'limi Saka, because he planted trees on Ochori land; the well folk are on the edge of the N'gomb forest, building huts and singing——"

"How long do they stay?" interrupted Hamilton.

"Lord, who knows?" said the man.

"Ogibo of the Akasava has spoken evilly of his king and mightily of himself——"

"Make a note of that, Bones?"

"Make a note of which, sir?"

"Ogibo—he looked like a case of sleep-sickness the last time I was in his village—go on."

"Ogibo also says that the father of his father was a great chief and was lord of all the Akasava——"

"That's sleeping sickness all right," said Hamilton bitterly. "Why the devil doesn't he wait till Sanders is back before he goes mad?"

"Drop him a line, sir," suggested Bones, "he's a remarkable feller—dash it all, sir, what the dooce is the good of bein' in charge of the district if you can't put a stop to that sort of thing?"

"What talk is there of spears in this?" asked Hamilton of the spy.

"Lord, much talk — as I know — for I serve in this district."

"Go swiftly to Ogibo, and summon him to me for a high *lakimbo*[1]," said Hamilton; "my soldiers shall carry you in my new little ship that burns water[2]—fly pigeons to me that I may know all that happens."

[1] Palaver. [2] The motor launch.

"On my life," said the spy, raised his hand in salute and departed.

"These well people you were talkin' about sir," asked Bones. "who are they?"

But Hamilton could give no satisfactory answer to such a question, and, indeed, he would have been more than ordinarily clever had he been able to.

The wild territories are filled with stubborn facts, bewildering realities, and extraordinary inconsequences. Up by the N'gombi lands lived a tribe who, for the purposes of office classification, were known as "N'gombi (Interior),"but who were neither N'gombi nor Isisi, nor of any known branch of the Bantu race, but known as "the people of the well." They had remarkable legends, sayings which they ascribed to a mythical I'doosi; also they have a song which runs:

> O well in the forest!
> Which chiefs have digged;
> No common men touched the earth,
> But chiefs' spears and the hands of kings.

Now there is no doubt that both the sayings of I'doosi and the song of the well have come down from days of antiquity, and that I'doosi is none other than the writer of the lost book of the Bible, of whom it is written:

"Now the rest of the acts of Solomon, first and last, are they not written in the history of Nathan the prophet, and in the prophecy of Ahijah the Shilonite, and in the vision of Idoo the seer?"[1]. . . .

And is not the Song of the Well identical with that brief extract from the Book of Wars of the Lord—lost to us for ever—which runs:

"Spring up, O well: sing ye unto it: The well, which the princes digged, Which the nobles of the people delved, With the sceptre . . . with their staves."[2]

[1] Chronicles II, ix. 29.
[2] Numbers, xxi. 17.

Some men say that the People of the Well are one of the lost tribes, but that is an easy solution which suggests itself to the hasty-minded. Others say that they are descendants of the Babylonian races, or that they came down from Egypt when Rameses II died, and there arose a new dynasty and a Pharaoh who did not know the wise Jewish Prime Minister who ruled so wisely, who worshipped in the little temple at Karnac, and whose statue you may see in Cairo with a strange Egyptian name. We know him better as "Joseph"—he who was sold into captivity.

Whatever they were, this much is known, to the discomfort of everybody, that they were great diggers of wells, and would, on the slightest excuse, spend whole months, choosing, for some mad reason, the top of hills for their operations, delving in the earth for water, though the river was less than a hundred yards away.

Of all the interesting solutions which have been offered with the object of identifying the People of the Well, none are so interesting as that which Bones put forward at the end of Hamilton's brief sketch.

"My idea, dear old officer," he said profoundly, "that all these Johnnies are artful old devils who've run away from their wives in Timbuctoo—and for this reason——"

"Oh, shut up!" said Hamilton.

Two nights later the bugles were ringing through the Houssa lines, and Bones, sleepy-eyed, with an armful of personal belongings, was racing for the *Zaire*, for Ogibo of the Akasava had secured a following.

II

The chief Ogibo who held the law and kept the peace for his master, the King of the Akasava, was bitten many times by the tsetse on a hunting trip into the bad lands near the Utur forest. Two years afterwards, of a sudden, he was seized with a sense of his own importance, and proclaimed himself paramount chief of the Akasava, and all the lands adjoining. And since it is against nature that any lunatic should be without his following, he had no difficulty in raising all the spears that were requisite for his immediate purpose, marched to Igili, the second most important town in the Akasava kingdom, overthrew the defensive force, destroyed the town, and leaving half his fighting regiment to hold the conquered city he moved through the forest toward the Akasava city proper. He camped in the forest, and his men spent an uncomfortable night, for a thunderstorm broke over the river, and the dark was filled with quick flashes and the heavens crashed noisily. There was still a rumbling and a growling above his head when he assembled his forces in the grey dawn, and continued his march. He had not gone half an hour before one of his headmen came racing up to where he led his force in majesty.

"Lord," said he, "do you hear no sound?"

"I hear the thunder," said Ogibo.

"Listen!" said the headman.

They halted, head bent.

"It is thunder," said Ogibo, as the rumble and moan of the distant storm came to him. Then above the grumble of the thunder came a sharper note, a sound to be expressed in the word "blong!"

"Lord," said the headman, "that is no thunder, rather is it the fire-thrower of M'ilitani."

So Ogibo in his wrath turned back to crush the insolent white men who had dared to attack the garrison he had left behind to hold Iglili.

Bones with a small force was pursuing him, totally unaware of the strength that Ogibo mustered. A spy brought to the chief news of the smallness of the following force.

"Now," said Ogibo, "I will show all the world how great

a chief I am, for my bravery I will destroy all these soldiers that are sent against me."

He chose his ambush well—though he had need to send scampering with squeals of terror half a hundred humble aliens who were at the moment of interruption digging a foolish well on the top of the hill where Ogibo was concealing his shaking force.

Bones with his Houssas saw how the path led up a tolerably steep hill—one of the few in the country—and groaned aloud, for he hated hills.

He was half-way up at the head of his men, when Ogibo on the summit gave the order. "Boma!" said he, which means kill, and three abreast, shields locked and spears gripped stomach high, the rebels charged down the path. Bones saw them coming and slipped out his revolver. There was no room to manœuvre his men, the path was fairly narrow, dense undergrowth masked each side.

He heard the yell, saw above the bush, which concealed the winding way, the dancing head-dresses of the attackers, and advanced his pistol arm. The rustle of bare feet on the path, a louder roar than ever—then silence.

Bones waited, a Houssa squeezed on either side of him, but the onrushing enemy did not appear, and only a faint whimper of sound reached him.

"Lord! they go back!" gasped his sergeant; and Bones saw to his amazement a little knot of men making their frantic way up the hill.

At first he suspected an ambush within an ambush, but it was unlikely; he could never be more at Ogibo's mercy than he had been.

Cautiously he felt his way up the hill path, a revolver in each hand.

He rounded a sharp corner of the path and saw . . .

A great square chasm yawned in the very centre of the pathway, the bushes on either side were buried under the

140

earth which the diggers of wells had flung up, and piled one on the other, a writhing, struggling confusion of shining bodies, were Ogibo's soldiers to the number of a hundred, with a silent Ogibo undermost, wholly indifferent to his embarrassing position, for his neck was broken.

Hamilton came up in the afternoon and brought villagers to assist at the work of rescue and afterwards he interviewed the chief of the shy and timid Well-folk.

"O chief," said Hamilton, "it is an order of Sandi that you shall dig no wells near towns, and yet you have done this."

"Bless his old heart!" murmured Bones.

"Lord, I break the law," said the man, simply, "also I break all custom, for to-day, by your favour, I cross the river, I and my people. This we have never done since time was."

"Whither do you go?"

The chief of the wanderers, an old man remarkably gifted —for his beard was long and white, and reached to his waist —stuck his spear head down in the earth.

"Lord, we go to a place which is written," he said; "for Idoosi has said, 'Go forth to the natives at war, they that fight by the river; on the swift water shall you go, even against the water'—many times have we come to the river, master, but ever have we turned back; but now it seems that the prophecy has been fulfilled, for there are bleeding men in these holes and the sound of thunders."

The People of the Well crossed to the Isisi, using the canoes of the Akasava headmen, and made a slow progress through territory which gave them no opportunity of exercising their hobby, since water lay less than a spade's length beneath the driest ground.

"Poor old Sanders," said Hamilton ruefully, when he was again on the *Zaire*, "I've so mixed up his people that he'll have to get a new map made to find them again."

"You might tell me off to show him round, sir," suggested Bones, but Hamilton did not jump at the offer.

He was getting more than a little rattled. Sanders was due back in a month, and it seemed that scarcely a week passed but some complication arose that further entangled a situation which was already too full of loose and straying threads for his liking.

"I suppose the country is settled for a week at any rate," he said with a little sigh of relief—but he reckoned without his People of the Well.

They moved, a straggling body of men and women, with their stiff walk and their doleful song, a wild people with strange, pinched faces and long black hair, along the river's edge.

A week's journeyings brought them to the Ochori country and to Bosambo, who was holding a most important palaver.

It was held on Ochori territory, for the forbidden strip was by this time so thickly planted with young trees that there was no place for a man to sit.

"Lord," said Bosambo, "if you will return me that land which you have stolen, so that I may pass unhindered from one part of my territory to the other, I will give you many islands on the river."

"That is a foolish palaver," said B'limisaka; "for you have no islands to give."

"Now I tell you, B'limisaka," said Bosambo, "my young men are crying out against you, for, as you know, you have planted your trees on the high ground, and my people, taking to their canoes, must climb down to the water's edge a long way, so that it wearies their legs, soon, I fear, I shall not hold them, for they are very fierce and full of arrogance."

"Lord," said B'limisaka, significantly, "my young men are also fierce."

The palaver was dispersing, and the last of the Lombobo councillors were disappearing in the forest, when the

142

Diggers of the Well came through the forbidden territory to the place where Bosambo sat.

"We are they of whom you have heard, O my Lord," said the old man, who led them, "also we carry a book for you."

He unwound the cloth about his thin middle, and with many fumblings produced a paper which Bosambo read.

"From M'ilitani, by Ogibo's village in the Akasava.

"To Bosambo—may God preserve him!

"I give this to the Chief of Well diggers that you shall know they are favoured by me, being simple people and very timid. Give them a passage through your territory, for they seek a holy land, and find them high places for the digging of holes, for they seek truth. Now peace on your house, Bosambo."

"On my ship, by channel of rocks."

"Lord, it is true," said the old chief, "we seek a shining thing that will stay white when it is white, and black when it is black, and the wise Idoosi has said, 'Go down into the earth for truth, seek it in the deeps of the earth, for it lies in secret places, in centre of the world it lies.'"

Bosambo thought long and rapidly, then there came to him the bright light of an inspiration.

"What manner of holes do you dig, old man?"

"Lord, we dig them deep, for we are cunning workers, and do not fear death as common men do; also we dig them straightly—into the very heart of hills we dig them."

Bosambo looked at the sloping ground covered with hateful gum.

"Old man," said he softly, "here shall you dig, you and your people, for in the heart of this hill is such a truth as you desire—my young men shall bring you food and build huts for you, and I will place one who is cunning in the way of hills to show you the way."

The old man's eyes gleamed joyously, and he clasped the ankles of his magnanimous host.

"Lord," said he humbly, "now is the prophecy fulfilled, for it was said by the great Idoosi, 'You shall come to a land where the barbarian rules, and he shall be to you as a brother!'"

"Wretch," said Bosambo in his vile English—yet with a certain hauteur, "you shall dig 'um tunnel—you no cheek 'um, no chat 'um, you lib for dear tunnel one time."

He watched them as, singing the song of the well, they went to work, women, men, and even little children undermining the Chief B'limisaka's territory and creating for Bosambo the right of way for which his soul craved.

CHAPTER IX

THE GREEN CROCODILE

Cala cala, as they say, seven brothers lived near the creek of the Green One. It was not called the creek of the Green One in those far-off days, for the monstrous thing had no existence.

And the seven brothers had seven wives who were sisters, and it would appear from the legend that these seven wives were unfaithful to their husbands, and upon a certain night in the full of the moon, the brothers returning from an expedition into the forest, discovered the extent of their infamy, and they tied the sisters together, the wrists of one to the ankles of the other, and they led them to the stream, and no sooner had they disappeared beneath the black waters than there was almighty splashing and bubbling of water, and there came crawling from the place where the unfaithful wives had sunk so terrible a monster that the seven brothers fled in fear.

This was the Green One, with his long ugly snout, cold, vicious eyes, and his great clawed feet. Some say that these women had been changed by magic into the Crocodile of the Pool, and many people believe this and speak of the Green One in the plural.

Certain it is, that this terrible crocodile lived through the ages—none hunting her, she was left in indisputable possession of the flat sand-bank wherein to lay her eggs, and ranged the sandy shore of the creek undisturbed.

She was regarded with awe; sacrifices, living and dead, were offered to her from time to time, and sometimes a cripple or two was knocked on the head and left by the water's edge for her pleasure. She was indeed a veritable scavenger of crime for the neighbouring villages about, and earned some sort of respect, for, as the saying went:

"Sandi does not speak the language of the Green One."

Sometimes M'zooba would go afield, leaving the quietude of the creek and the pool, which was her own territory, for the more adventurous life of the river, and here one day she lay, the whole of her body submerged and only her wicked eyes within an eighth of an inch of the water's surface, when a timorous young roebuck came picking a cautious way through the forest across the open plantations to the water's edge. He stopped from time to time apprehensively, trembling in every limb at the slightest sound, looking this way and that, then taking a few more steps and again searching the cruel world for danger before he reached the water's edge.

Then, after a final look round, he lowered his soft muzzle to the cool waters. Swift as lightning the Green One flashed her long snout out of the water, and gripped the tender head of the buck. Ruthlessly she pulled, dragging the struggling deer after her till first its neck and then its shoulders, then finally the last frantic waving stump of its white tail went under the dark waters.

Out in midstream a white little boat was moving steadily up the river and on the awning-shaded bridge an indignant

B.—K

young man witnessed the tragedy. The Green One had her larder under a large shelving rock half a dozen feet beneath the water. Into this cavity her long hard nose flung her dead victim, and her four powerful hands covered the entrance to the water cave with sand and rock. More than satisfied with her morning's work, the Green One came to the surface of the water to bask in the glowing warmth of the morning sunlight.

She took a survey upon the world, made up of low-lying shores and a hot blue sky. She saw a river, broad and oily, and a strange white object which she had seen often before smoking towards her.

And that was the last thing she ever saw; for Bones, on the bridge of the *Zaire*, squinted along the sights of his Express and pressed the trigger. Struck in the head by an explosive bullet, the Green One went out in a flurry of stormy water.

"Thus perish all rotten old crocodiles," said Bones, immensely pleased with himself, and he placed the rifle on the rack.

"What the devil are you shooting at, so early in the morning?" asked Hamilton.

He came out in his pyjamas, sun helmet on his head, pliant mosquito boots reaching to his knees.

"A crocodile, sir," said Bones.

"Why waste good ammunition on crocodiles?" asked Hamilton; "was it something exceptional?"

"A tremendous chap, sir," said the enthusiastic Bones, "some fifty feet long, and as green as——"

"As green!" repeated Hamilton quickly, "where are we?"

He looked with a swift glance along the shore for landmarks.

"I hope to goodness you have not shot old M'zooba," he said.

146

"I don't know your friend by name," said Bones, "but why shouldn't I shoot him?"

"Because, you silly ass," said Hamilton, "she is a sort of sacred crocodile."

"She was never so sacred as she is now, sir, for:

"She's flapping her wings in the crocodile heaven," said Bones, flippantly; "for I'm one of those dead shots—once I draw a bead on an animal——"

"Get out a canoe and set the woodmen to dive for the Green One," said Hamilton to his orderly, for a shot crocodile invariably sinks to the bottom and can only be recovered by diving.

They brought it to the surface, and Hamilton groaned.

"It is M'zooba," he said in resigned exasperation. "Oh, Bones, what an ass you are!"

Bones said nothing, but walked to the stern of the ship and lowered the blue ensign to half-mast—a piece of impertinence which Hamilton did not discover till a long time afterwards.

Now whatever might be the desire or wish of Hamilton and however much he might on ordinary occasions depend upon the loyalty of his warders and his men, in this matter of the green crocodile he was entirely at their mercy, for he could not call them together asking them to speak on death of the Green One without magnifying the importance of Lieutenant Tibbett's rash act. The only attitude he could adopt was to treat the Green One and her untimely end as something which was in the day's work neither to be lamented nor acclaimed, and when, at the first village, a doleful deputation, comprising a worried chief and a sulky witch-doctor, called upon him to bemoan the tragedy, he treated the matter with great joviality.

"For what is a crocodile more or less in this river?" he asked.

"Lord, this was no crocodile," said the witch-doctor,

"but a very reverend ghost, and it has been our Ju-ju for many years, bringing us good crops and fair weather for our goodness, and has eaten up all the devils and sickness which came to our villages. Now it is gone nothing but ill-fortune can come to us."

"Bugobo," said Hamilton, "you talk like a foolish one, for how may a crocodile who does not leave the water, and, moreover, is evil and old, a stealer of women and children and dangerous to your goats, how can this thing bring good fortune to any people?"

"How can the river run, lord?" replied the man, "and yet it does."

Hamilton thought for a moment.

"Now I tell you this, and you shall say to all people who ask you, that by my magic I will bring another green one to this stream, greater and larger than the one who has gone, and she shall be ju-ju for all men."

"And now," he said to Bones, when the deputation had left, "it is up to you to go out and find a nice, respectable crocodile to take the place of the lady you have so light-heartedly destroyed."

Bones gasped.

"Dear old feller," he said feebly, "the habits and customs of fauna of this land are entirely beyond me. I will fetch you a crocodile, sir, with the greatest of pleasure, although as far as I know there is nothing laid down in the King's regulations of the warrants for pay and promotion defining the catching of crocodiles as part of an officer's duty."

Hamilton made no further move towards replacing the lost Spirit of the Pool until he learnt that his offer had been taken very seriously, and that the coming of the great new Green One to the pool, was a subject of discussion up and down the river.

Now here is a fact which official records go to substantiate. Although the "Reports of the Territories" take

148

no cognisance of ghosts and spirits and other occult influence, dealing rather with such mundane facts as the condition of crops and the discipline of the races, yet the reports of that particular year in this one district made gloomy reading both for Hamilton and for the Administrator in his far-off stone house.

Though the crops throughout the whole of the country were good that Hamilton was apprehensive about the consequences—for men fight better with a full larder behind them—yet in this immediate neighbourhood of the pool, within its sphere of influence, so to speak, the crops failed miserably, and the fish which haunt the shallow stream beneath the big stream near the channel took it into their silly heads to migrate to other distant waters. Here, then, was the consequence of Bones' murder demonstrated to a most alarming extent. There was a blight in the potatoes; the maize crop, for some unaccountable reason, was a meagre one; there were three unexpected cases of sleeping sickness followed by madness in an interior village, and, crowning disaster of all, one of those sudden storms which sweep across the river came upon the village, and lightning struck the huts.

"My son," said Hamilton, when they brought the news to him, "you have got to go out and find a green crocodile, quick."

So Bones went up the river with the naphtha launch, leaving to Hamilton the delicate task of finding a natural explanation for all the horrors which had come upon the unfortunate people.

Green crocodiles are rare even on the great river which had half a million other kinds of crocodiles to its credit, for green is both a sign of age, and by common report indicative of cannibalistic tendencies.

In whatever veneration the Green One of the Pool might be held, such respect did not extend to other parts of the river, where the green ones were sought out and slain in their early youth. Bones spent an exciting seven days chasing, lassoing and, at times in self-defence, shooting at great reptiles without getting any nearer to the object of his search.

"Ahmet," said he, in despair, "it seems that there are no green crocodiles on this river."

"Lord, there are very few," admitted the man; "for the people kill green crocodiles owing to their evil influence."

At every village there was news for Bones which lightened his heart. Someone had seen such a monster, it lived in a pool or lorded some creek, generally only get-at-able in a canoe; and here Bones, with his Houssas, would wait smoking furiously, with baited lines cunningly laid from thick underbush or some tethered goat, bleating invitingly on the banks. But never once did the hunter catch so much as a glimpse of green. There were yellow crocodiles, grey crocodiles, crocodiles the colour of the sand, or the dark-brown bed of the river, but nothing which by any stretch of imagination could be called green.

And urgent messages came to Bones. The *Zaire* itself, in charge of Abiboo, came steaming up carrying a letter filled with unnecessary abuse, for Hamilton was getting rattled by the extraordinary manifestations which he received every day of the potency of this slain monster. Bones sent the sergeant back in the launch with an insubordinate message, and commandeered the *Zaire* with her superior accommodation for himself.

"There is only one thing to do," he said, "and that is to consult jolly old Bosambo."

So he put the head of the *Zaire* to the Ochori country, and on the second day arrived at the city.

"Lord," said Bosambo, loftily, "crocodiles I have by thousands."

150

"Green ones?" asked Bones anxiously.

"Lord, of every colour," said Bosambo, "blue or green or red, even golden crocodiles have I in my splendid river. But they will cost great money because they are very cunning, and my hunters of crocodiles are independent men who do not care to work."

Bones dried up the flood of eloquence quickly.

"O Bosambo," said he, "there is no money for this palaver, but a green crocodile I must have because the evil people of the Lower Isisi say I have put a spell on their land because I slew the Green One, M'zooba, also this crocodile must I have before the moon is due. My Lord M'ilitani has sent me many powerful messages to this effect."

This was another matter, and Bosambo looked dubious.

"Lord," said he, "what manner of green was this crocodile, for I never saw it?"

Bones looked round.

Neither the green of the trees he saw, nor the green of the grass underfoot, nor the green of the elephant grass growing strongly on the river's edge, nor the tender green of the high trees above, nor the tender green of the young Isisi palms; and yet the exact shade of green it was necessary to secure. He ransacked all his books, turned over all his possessions and Hamilton's too, in an endeavour to match the crocodile. There was a suit of pyjamas of Hamilton's which had a stripe very near, but not quite.

"Oh Ahmet," said Bones at last in desperation, "go to the storeman, and let him bring all the paints he has so that I may show Bosambo a certain colour."

They found the exact shade at last on a ten-pound tin of Aspinall enamels, and Bosambo thought long.

"Lord," said he, "I think I know where I may find just such a crocodile as you want."

Late that night Bones met Bosambo before his hut in a

long and earnest palaver, and an hour before dawn he went out with Bosambo and his huntsmen, and was pulled to a certain creek in the Ochori land which is notorious for the size and strength of its crocodiles.

II

No doubt but Hamilton had a serious task before him, for although the grievance which he had to allay was limited to the restricted area over which the spirit of M'zooba brooded, yet the people of the crocodile had many sympathisers who resented as bitterly as the affected parties this interference with what Downing Street called "local religious customs."

A wholly unauthorised palaver was held in the forest which was attended by delegations from the Akasava and the N'gombi, and spies brought the news to Hamilton that the little witch-doctors were going through the villages carrying stories of desolation which had come as the result of M'zooba's death.

The palaver Hamilton dispensed with some brusqueness. Twenty soldiers and a machine-gun were uninvited guests to the gathering, and the meeting retired in disorder. Two of the witch-doctors Hamilton's men caught. One he flogged with all the village looking on, and the other he sent to the Village of Irons for twelve months.

And all the time he spoke of the newer green one which was coming, which his magic would invoke, and which would surely appear "tied by one leg" to a stake near the pool, for all men to see.

He founded a sect of new-green-one worshippers (quite unwittingly). It needed only the corporeal presence of his novel deity to wipe out the feelings of distrust which violence had not wholly dispelled.

Day after day passed, but no word came from Bones, and Captain Hamilton cursed his subordinate, his subordinate's relations, and all the cruelty of fate which brought Bones into his command. Then, unexpectantly, the truant arrived, arrived proud and triumphant in the early morning before Hamilton was awake. He sneaked into the village so quietly that even the Houssa sentry who dozed across the threshold of Hamilton's hut was not aware of his return; and silently, with fiercely whispered injunctions, so that the surprise should be all the more complete, Bones landed his unruly cargo, its feet chained, his great muzzle lassoed and bound with raw hide, its powerful and damaging tail firmly fixed between two planks of wood (a special idea for which Bones was responsible). Then Lieutenant Tibbetts went to the hut of his chief and woke him.

"So here you are, are you?" said Hamilton.

"I am here," said Bones with trembling pride, so that Hamilton knew his subordinate had been successful; "according to your instructions, sir, I have captured the green crocodile. He is of monstrous size, and vastly superior to your partly-worn lady friend. Also," he said, "as per your instructions, conveyed to me in your letter dated the twenty-third instant, I have fastened same by right leg in the vicinity of the pool; at least," he corrected carefully, "he was fastened, but owing to certain technical difficulties, he slipped cable, so to speak, and is wallowing in his native element."

"You are not rotting, Bones, are you?" asked Hamilton, busy with his toilet.

"Perfectly true and sound, sir, I never rot," said Bones stiffly; "give me a job of work to do, give me a task, put me upon my mettle, sir, and with the assistance of jolly old Bosambo——"

"Is Bosambo in this?"

Bones hesitated.

"He assisted me very considerably, sir," he said; "but, so to speak, the main idea was mine."

The chief's drum summoned the villages to the palaver house, but the news had already filtered through the little township, and a crowd had gathered waiting eagerly to hear the message which Hamilton had to give them.

"O people," he said, addressing them from the hill of palaver, "all I have promised you I have performed. Behold now in the pool—and you shall come with me to see this wonder—is one greater than M'zooba, a vast and splendid spirit which shall protect your crops and be as M'zooba was, and better than was M'zooba. All this I have done for you."

"Lord Tibbetti has done for you," prompted Bones, in a hoarse whisper.

"All this I have done for you," repeated Hamilton firmly, "because I love you."

He led the way through the broad, straggling plantation to the great pool which begins in a narrow creek leading from the river and ends in a sprawl of water to the east of the village.

The whole countryside stood about watching the still water, but nothing happened.

"Can't you whistle him and make him come up or something?" asked Hamilton.

"Sir," said an indignant Bones, "I am no crocodile tamer; willing as I am to oblige you, and clever as I am with parlour tricks, I have not yet succeeded in inducing a crocodile to come to heel after a week's acquaintance."

But native people are very patient.

They stood or squatted, watching the unmoved surface of the water for half an hour, and then suddenly there was a stir and a little gasp of pleasurable apprehension ran through the assembly.

Then slowly the new one came up. He made for a

154

sand-bank, which showed above the water in the centre of the pool; first his snout, then his long body emerged from the water, and Hamilton gasped.

"Good heavens, Bones!" he said in a startled whisper, and his astonishment was echoed from a thousand throats.

And well might he be amazed at the spectacle which the complacent Bones had secured for him.

For this great reptile was more than green, he was a green so vivid that it put the colours of the forest to shame. A bright, glittering green and along the centre of his broad back one zig-zag splash of orange.

"Phew," whistled Hamilton, "this is something like."

The roar of approval from the people was unmistakable. The crocodile turned his evil head and for a moment, as it seemed to Bones, his eyes glinted viciously in the direction of the young and enterprising officer. And Bones admitted after to a feeling of panic.

Then with a malignant "woof!" like the hoarse, growling bark of a dog, magnified a hundred times, he slid back into the water, a great living streak of vivid green and disappeared to the cool retreat at the bottom of the pool.

"You have done splendidly, Bones, splendidly," said Hamilton, and clapped him on the back; "really you are a most enterprising devil."

"Not at all, sir," said Bones.

He ate his dinner on the *Zaire*, answering with monosyllables the questions which Hamilton put to him regarding the quest and the place of the origin of this wonderful beast. It was after dinner when they were smoking their cigars in the gloom as the *Zaire* was steaming across its way to the shore where a wooding offered an excuse for a night's stay, and Bones gave voice to his thoughts.

And curiously enough his conversation did not deal directly or indirectly with his discovery.

"When was this boat decorated last, sir?" he asked.

"About six months before Sanders left," replied Hamilton in surprise; "just why do you ask?"

"Nothing, sir," said Bones, and whistled lightheartedly. Then he returned to the subject.

"I only asked you because I thought the enamel work in the cabin and all that sort of thing has worn very well."

"Yes, it is good wearing stuff," said Hamilton.

"That green paint in the bathroom is rather *chic*, isn't it? Is that good wearing stuff?"

"The enamel?" smiled Hamilton. "Yes, I believe that is very good wearing. I am not a whale on domestic matters, Bones, but I should imagine that it would last for another year without showing any sign of wear."

"Is it waterproof at all?" asked Bones, after another pause.

"What do you mean?"

"I mean would it wash off if a lot of water were applied to it?"

"No, I should not imagine it would," said Hamilton, "what makes you ask?"

"Oh, nothing!" said Bones carelessly and whistled, looking up to the stars that were peeping from the sky; and the inside of Lieutenant Tibbetts was one large expansive grin.

CHAPTER X

HENRY HAMILTON BONES

LIEUTENANT FRANCIS AUGUSTUS TIBBETTS of the Houssas was at some disadvantage with his chief and friend. Lieutenant F. A. Tibbetts might take a perfectly correct attitude, might salute on every possible occasion that a man could salute, might click his heels together in the German fashion (he had spent a year at Heidelberg), might be stiffly formal and so greet his superior that he contrived to combine a dutiful recognition with the cut direct, but never could he overcome one fatal obstacle to marked avoidance—he had to grub with Hamilton.

Bones was hurt. Hamilton had behaved to him as no brother officer should behave. Hamilton had spoken harshly and cruelly in the matter of a commission with which he had entrusted his subordinate, and with which the aforesaid subordinate had lamentably failed to cope.

Up in the Akasava country a certain wise man named M'bisibi had predicted the coming of a devil-child who should be born on a night when the moon lay so on the river and certain rains had fallen in the forest.

And this child should be called "Ewa," which is death; and first his mother would die and then his father; and he would grow up to be a scourge to his people and a pestilence to his nation, and crops would wither when he walked past them, and the fish in the river would float belly up in stinking death, and until Ewa M'faba himself went out, nothing but ill-fortune should come to the N'gombi–Isisi.

Thus M'bisibi predicted, and the word went up and down the river, for the prophet was old and accounted wise even by Bosambo of the Ochori.

It came to Hamilton quickly enough, and he had sent Bones post-haste to await the advent of any unfortunate youngster who was tactless enough to put in an appearance at such an inauspicious moment as would fulfil the prediction of M'bisibi.

And Bones had gone to the wrong village, and that in the face of his steersman's and his sergeant's protest that he was going wrong. Fortunately, by reliable account, no child had been born in the village, and the prediction was unfulfilled.

"Otherwise," said Hamilton, "its young life would have been on your head."

"Yes, sir," said Bones.

"I didn't tell you there were two villages called Inkau," Hamilton confessed, "because I didn't realise you were chump enough to go to the wrong one."

"No, sir," agreed Bones, patiently.

"Naturally," said Hamilton, "I thought the idea of saving the lives of innocent babes would have been sufficient incentive."

"Naturally, sir," said Bones, with forced geniality.

"I've come to one conclusion about you, Bones," said Hamilton.

"Yes, sir," said Bones, "that I'm an ass, sir, I think?"

Hamilton nodded—it was too hot to speak.

"It was an interestin' conclusion," said Bones, thoughtfully, "not without originality—when it first occurred to you, but as a conclusion, if you will pardon my criticism, sir, if you will forgive me for suggestin' as much—in callin' me an ass, sir: apart from its bein' contrary to the spirit an' letter of the Army Act—God Save the King!—it's a bit low, sir." And he left his superior officer without another word. For three days they sat at breakfast, tiffin and dinner, and neither said more than:

"May I pass you the bread, sir?"

"Thank you sir; have you the salt, sir?"

Hamilton was so busy a man that he might have forgotten the feud, but for the insistence of Bones, who never lost an opportunity of reminding his No. 1 that he was mortally hurt.

One night, dinner had reached the stage where two young officers of Houssas sat primly side by side on the verandah sipping their coffee. Neither spoke, and the seance might have ended with the conventional "Good night" and that punctilious salute which Bones invariably gave, and which

158

Hamilton as punctiliously returned, but for the apparition of a dark figure which crossed the broad space of parade ground hesitatingly as though not certain of his way, and finally came with dragging feet through Sanders' garden to the edge of the verandah.

It was the figure of a small boy, very thin; Hamilton could see this through the half-darkness.

The boy was as naked as when he was born, and he carried in his hand a single paddle.

"O boy," said Hamilton, "I see you."

"Wanda!" said the boy in a frightened tone, and hesitated, as though he were deciding whether it would be better to bolt, or to conclude his desperate enterprise.

"Come up to me," said Hamilton, kindly.

He recognised by the dialect that the visitor had come a long way, as indeed he had, for his old canoe was pushed up amongst the elephant grass a mile away from headquarters, and he had spent three days and nights upon the river. He came up, an embarrassed and a frightened lad, and stood twiddling his toes on the unaccustomed smoothness of the big stoep.

"Where do you come from, and why have you come?" asked Hamilton.

"Lord, I have come from the village of M'bisibi," said the boy; "my mother has sent me because she fears for her life, my father being away on a great hunt. As for me," he went on, "my name is Tilimi-N'kema."

"Speak on, Tilimi the Monkey," said Hamilton, "tell me why the woman your mother fears for her life."

The boy was silent for a spell; evidently he was trying to recall the exact formula which had been dinned into his unreceptive brain, and to repeat word for word the lesson which he had learned parrotwise.

"Thus says the woman my mother," he said at last, with the blank, monotonous delivery peculiar to all small boys who have been rehearsed in speech, "on a certain day when the moon was at full and the rain was in the forest so that we all heard it in the village, my mother bore a child who is my own brother, and, lord, because she feared things which the old man M'bisibi had spoken she went into the forest to a certain witch-doctor, and there the child was born. To my mind," said the lad, with a curious air of wisdom which is the property of the youthful native from whom none of the mysteries of life or death are hidden, "it is better she did this, for they would have made a sacrifice of her child. Now when she came back, and they spoke to her, she said that the boy was dead. But this is the truth, lord, that she had left this child with the witch-doctor, and now——" he hesitated again.

"And now?" repeated Hamilton.

"Now, lord," said the boy, "this witch-doctor, whose name is Bogolono, says she must bring him rich presents at the full of every moon, because her son and my brother is the devil-child whom M'bisibi has predicted. And if she brings no rich presents he will take the child to the village, and there will be an end."

Hamilton called his orderly.

"Give this boy some chop," he said; "tomorrow we will have a longer palaver."

He waited till the man and his charge were out of earshot, then he turned to Bones.

"Bones," he said, seriously, "I think you had better leave unobtrusively for M'bisibi's village, find the woman, and bring her to safety. You will know the village," he added, unnecessarily, "it is the one you didn't find last time."

Bones left insubordinately and made no response.

Bosambo, with his arms folded across his brawny chest, looked curiously at the deputation which had come to him.

"This is a bad palaver," said Bosambo, "for it seems to me that when little chiefs do that which is wrong, it is an ill thing; but when great kings, such as your master Iberi, stand at the back of such wrongdoings, that is the worst thing of all, and though this M'bisibi is a wise man, as we all know, and indeed the only wise man of your people, has brought out this devil-child, and makes a killing palaver, then M'ilitani will come very quickly with his soldiers and there will be an end to little chiefs and big chiefs alike."

"Lord, that will be so," said the messenger, "unless all chiefs in the land stand in brotherhood together. And because we know Sandi loves you, and M'ilitani also, and that Tibbetti himself is as tender to you as a brother, M'bisibi sent this word saying, 'Go to Bosambo, and say M'bisibi, the wise man, bids him come to a great and fearful palaver touching the matter of several devils. Tell him also that great evil will come to this land, to his land and to mine, to his wife and the wives of his counsellors, and to his children and theirs, unless we make an end to certain devils.'"

Bosambo, chin on clenched fist, looked thoughtfully at the other.

"This cannot be," said he in a troubled voice; "for though I die and all that is wonderful to me shall pass out of this world, yet I must do no thing which is unlawful in the eyes of Sandi, my master, and of the great ones he has left behind to fulfil the law. Say this to M'bisibi from me, that I think he is very wise and understands ghosts and such-like palavers. Also say that if he puts curses upon my huts I will come with my spearmen to him, and if aught follows I will hang him by the ears from a high tree, though he sleeps with ghosts and commands whole armies of devils; this palaver is finished."

The messenger carried the word back to M'bisibi and the council of the chiefs and the elder men who sat in the palaver house, and old as he was and wise by all standards, M'bisibi shivered, for, as he explained, that which Bosambo said would he do. For this is peculiar to no race or colour, that old men love life dearer than young.

"Bongolono, you shall bring the child," he said, turning to one who sat at his side, string upon string of human teeth looped about his neck and his eyes circled with white ashes, "and it shall be sacrificed according to the custom, as it was in the days of my fathers and of their fathers."

They chose a spot in the forest, where four young trees stood at corners of a rough square. With their short bush knives they lopped the tender branches away, leaving four plaint poles that bled stickily. With great care they drew down the tops of these trees until they nearly met, cutting the heads so that there was no overlapping. To these four ends they fastened ropes, one for each arm and for each ankle of the devil child, and with other ropes they held the saplings to their place.

"Now this is the magic of it," said M'bisibi, "that when the moon is full tonight, we shall sacrifice first a goat, and then a fowl, casting certain parts into the fire which shall be made of white gum, and I will make certain marks upon the child's face and upon his belly, and then I will cut these ropes so that to the four ends of the world we shall cast forth this devil, who will no longer trouble us."

That night came many chiefs, Iberi of the Akasava, Tilini of the Lesser Isisi, Efele (the Tornado) of the N'gombi, Lisu (the Seer) of the Inner Territories, but Lilongo[1] (as they called Bosambo of the Ochori), did not come.

---

[1] "Lilongo" is from the noun "balongo"—blood, and means literally "he-who-breaks-blood-friendships."—E.W.

Bones reached the village two hours before the time of sacrifice and landed a force of twenty Houssas and a small Maxin gun. The village was peaceable, and there was no sign of anything untoward. Save this. The village was given over to old people and children. M'bisibi was an hour—two hours—four hours in the forest. He had gone north—east—south—none knew whither.

The very evasiveness of the replies put Bones into a fret. He scouted the paths and found indications of people having passed over all three.

He sent his gun back to the *Zaire*, divided his party into three, and accompanied by half a dozen men, he himself took the middle path.

For an hour he trudged, losing his way, and finding it again. He came upon a further division of paths and split up his little force again.

In the end he found himself alone, struggling over the rough ground in a darkness illuminated only by the electric lamp he carried, and making for a faint gleam of red light which showed through the trees ahead.

M'bisibi held the child on his outstretched hands, a fat little child, with large, wondering eyes that stared solemnly at the dancing flames, and sucked a small brown thumb contentedly.

"Behold this child, oh chiefs and people," said M'bisibi, "who was born as I predicted, and is filled with devils!"

The baby turned his head so that his fat little neck was all rolled and creased, and said "Ah!" to the pretty fire and chuckled.

"Even now the devils speak," said M'bisibi, "but presently you shall hear them screaming through the world because I have scattered them," and he made his way to the bowed saplings.

163

Bones, his face scratched and bleeding, his uniform torn in a dozen places, came swiftly after him.

"My bird, I think," said Bones, and caught the child unscientifically.

Picture Bones with a baby under his arm—a baby indignant, outraged, infernally uncomfortable, and grimacing a yell into being.

"Lord," said M'bisibi, breathing quickly, "what do you seek?"

"That which I have," said Bones, waving him off with the black muzzle of his automatic Colt. "Tomorrow you shall answer for many crimes."

He backed quickly to the cover of the woods, scenting the trouble that was coming.

He heard the old man's roar.

"O people . . . this white man will loose devils upon the land!"

Then a throwing spear snicked the trunk of a tree, and another, for there were no soldiers, and this congregation of exorcisers were mad with wrath at the thought of the evil which Tibbetti was preparing for them.

"Snick!"

A spear struck Bones' boot.

"Shut your eyes, baby," said Bones, and fired into the brown. Then he ran for his life. Over roots and fallen trees he fell and stumbled, his tiny passenger yelling desperately.

"Oh, shut up!" snarled Bones, "what the dickens are you shouting about—hey? Haven't I saved your young life, you ungrateful little devil?"

Now and again he would stop to consult his illuminated compass. That the pursuit continued he knew, but he had the dubious satisfaction of knowing, too, that he had left the path and was in the forest.

Then he heard a faint shot, and another, and another, and grinned.

164

His pursuers had stumbled upon a party of Houssas.

From sheer exhaustion the baby had fallen asleep. Babies were confoundedly heavy—Bones had never observed the fact before, but with the strap of his sword belt he fashioned a sling that relieved him of some of the weight.

He took it easier now, for he knew M'bisibi's men would be frightened off. He rested for half an hour on the ground, and then came a snuffling leopard walking silently through the forest, betraying his presence only by the two green danger-lamps of his eyes.

Bones sat up and flourished his lamp upon the startled beast, which growled in fright, and went scampering through the forest like the great cat that he was.

The growl woke Bones' charge, and he awoke hungry and disinclined to further sleep without that inducement and comfort which his nurse was in no position to offer, whereupon Bones snuggled the whimpering child.

"He's a wicked old leopard!" he said, "to come and wake a child at this time of the night."

The knuckle of Bones' little finger soothed the baby, though it was a poor substitute for the nutriment it had every right to expect, and it whimpered itself to sleep.

Lieutenant Tibbetts looked at his compass again. He had located the shots to eastward, but he did not care to make a bee-line in that direction for fear of falling upon some of the enemy, whom he knew would be, at this time, making their way to the river.

For two hours before dawn he snatched a little sleep, and was awakened by a fierce tugging at his nose. He got up, laid the baby on the soft ground, and stood with arms akimbo, and his monocle firmly fixed, surveying his noisy companion.

"What the dooce are you making all this row about?" he asked indignantly. "Have a little patience, young feller, exercise a little *suaviter in modo*, dear old baby!"

But still the fat little morsel on the ground continued his noisy monologue, protesting in a language which is of an age rather than of a race, against the cruelty and the thoughtlessness and the distressing lack of consideration which his elder and better was showing him.

"I suppose you want some grub," said Bones, in dismay; and looked round helplessly.

He searched the pocket of his haversack, and had the good fortune to find a biscuit; his vacuum flask had just half a cup of warm tea. He fed the baby with soaked biscuit and drank the tea himself.

"You ought to have a bath or something," said Bones, severely; but it was not until an hour later that he found a forest pool in which to perform the ablution.

At three o'clock in the afternoon, as near as he could judge, for his watch had stopped, he struck a path, and would have reached the village before sundown, but for the fact that he again missed the path, and learnt of this fact about the same time as he discovered he had lost his compass.

Bones looked dismally at the wide-awake child.

"Dear old companion in arms," he said, gloomily, "we are lost."

The baby's face creased in a smile.

"It's nothing to laugh about, you silly ass," said Bones.

IV

"Master, of our Lord Tibbetti I do not know," said M'bisibi sullenly.

"Yet you shall know before the sun is black," said Hamilton, "and your young men shall find him, or there is a tree for you, old man, a quick death by *Ewa!*"

"I have sought, my lord," said M'bisibi, "all my hunters have searched the forest, yet we have not found him. A certain devil-pot is here."

166

He fumbled under a native cloth and drew forth Bones' compass.

"This only could we find on the forest path that leads to Inilaki."

"And the child is with him?"

"So men say," said M'bisibi, "though by my magic I know that the child will die, for how can a white man who knows nothing of little children give him life and comfort? Yet," he amended carefully, since it was necessary to preserve the character of the intended victim, "if this child is indeed a devil child, as I believe, he will lead my lord Tibbetti to terrible places and return himself unharmed."

"He will lead you to a place more terrible," said M'ilitani, significantly, and sent a nimble climber into the trees to fasten a block and tackle to a stout branch, and thread a rope through.

It was so effective that M'bisibi, an old man, became most energetically active. *Lokali* and swift messengers sent his villages to the search. Every half-hour the Hotchkiss gun of the *Zaire* banged noisily; and Hamilton, tramping through the woods, felt his heart sink as hour after hour passed without news of his comrade.

"I tell you this, lord," said the headman, who accompanied him, "that I think Tibbetti is dead and the child also. For this wood is filled with ghosts and savage beasts, also many strong and poisonous snakes. See, lord!" He pointed.

They had reached a clearing where the grass was rich and luxuriant, where overshadowing branches formed an idealic bower, where heavy white waxen flowers were looped from branch to branch holding the green boughs in their parasitical clutch. Hamilton followed the direction of his eyes. In the middle of the clearing was a long, sinuous shape, dark-brown, and violently coloured with patches of green and vermilion, that was swaying backward and forward, hissing angrily at some object before it.

"Good God!" said Hamilton, and dropped his hand on his revolver, but before it was clear of his holster, there came a sharp crack, and the snake leapt up and fell back as a bullet went snip-snapping through the undergrowth. Then Hamilton saw Bones. Bones in his shirtsleeves, bareheaded, his big pipe in his mouth, who came hurriedly through the trees pistol in hand.

"Naughty boy!" he said, reproachfully, and stooping, picked up a squalling brown object from the ground. "Didn't Daddy tell you not to go near those horrid snakes? Daddy spank you——"

Then he caught sight of the amazed Hamilton, clutched the baby in one hand, and saluted with the other.

"Baby present and correct, sir," he said, formally.

*　　*　　*　　*　　*

"What are you going to do with it?" asked Hamilton, after Bones had indulged in the luxury of a bath and had his dinner.

"Do with what, sir?" asked Bones.

"With this."

Hamilton pointed to a crawling morsel who was at that moment looking up to Bones for approval.

"What do you expect me to do, sir?" asked Bones, stiffly; "the mother is dead and he has no father. I feel a certain amount of responsibility about Henry."

"And who the dickens is Henry?" asked Hamilton.

Bones indicated the child with a fine gesture.

"Henry Hamilton Bones, sir," he said grandly. "The child of the regiment," he went on; "adopted by me to be a prop for my declining years, sir."

"Heaven and earth!" said Hamilton, breathlessly.

He went aft to recover his nerve, and returned to become an unseen spectator to a purely domestic scene, for Bones had immersed the squalling infant in his own india-rubber bath, and was gingerly cleaning him with a mop.

CHAPTER XI

BONES AT M'FA

HAMILTON of the Houssas coming down to headquarters met Bosamba by appointment at the junction of the rivers.

"O Bosambo," said Hamilton, "I have sent for you to make a *likambo* because of certain things which my other eyes have seen and my other ears have heard."

To some men this hint of report from the spies of Government might bring dismay and apprehension, but to Bosambo, whose conscience was clear, they awakened only curiosity.

"Lord, I am your eyes in the Ochori," he said with truth, "and God knows I report faithfully."

Hamilton nodded. He was yellow with fever, and the hand that filled the briar pipe shook with ague. All this Bosambo saw.

"It is not of you I speak, nor of your people, but of the Akasava and the N'gombi and the evil little men who live in the forest—now is it true that they speak mockingly of my lord Tibbetti?"

Bosambo hesitated.

"Lord," said he, "what dogs are they, that they should speak of the mighty? Yet I will not lie to you, M'ilitani: they mock Tibbetti, because he is young and his heart is pure."

Hamilton nodded again, and stuck out his jaw in troubled meditation.

"I am a sick man," he said, "and I must rest, sending Tibbetti to watch the river, because the crops are good and there is fish for all men, and because the people are prosperous, for, Bosambo, in such times there is much boastfulness, and the tribes are ripe for foolish deeds deserving to appear wonderful in the eyes of woman."

"All this I know, M'ilitani," said Bosambo, "and because you are sick, my heart and my stomach are sore. For though I do not love you as I love Sandi, who is more clever than you, yet I love you well enough to grieve. And Tibbetti also——"

He paused.

"He is young," said Hamilton, "and not yet grown to himself—now you, Bosambo, shall check men who are insolent to his face, and be to him as a strong right hand."

"On my head and my life," said Bosambo, "yet, lord M'ilitani, I think that his day will find him, for it is written in the Sura of the Djin that all men are born three times, and the day will come when Bonzi will be born again."

He was in his canoe before Hamilton realised what he had said.

"Tell me, Bosambo," said he, leaning over the side of the *Zaire*, "what name did you call my lord Tibbetti?"

"Bonzi," said Bosambo, innocently, "for such I have heard you call him."

"Oh, dog of a thief!" stormed Hamilton. "If you speak without respect of Tibbetti, I will break your head."

Bosambo looked up with a glint in his big, black eyes.

"Lord," he said softly, "it is said on the river 'speak only the words which high ones speak, and you can say no wrong,' and if you, who are wiser than any, call my lord 'Bonzi'—what goat am I that I should not call him 'Bonzi' also?"

Hamilton saw the canoe drift round, saw the flashing paddles dip regularly, and the chant of the Ochori boat song came fainter and fainter as Bosambo's state canoe began its long journey northward.

Hamilton reached headquarters with a temperature of 105, and declined Bones' well-meant offers to look after him.

"What you want, dear old officer," said Bones, fussing around, "is careful nursin'. Trust old Bones and he'll pull you back to health, sir. Keep up your pecker, sir, an' I'll bring you back so to speak from the valley of the shadow —go to bed an' I'll have a mustard plaster on your chest in half a jiffy."

"If you come anywhere near me with a mustard plaster," said Hamilton, pardonably annoyed, "I'll brain you!"

"Don't you think!" asked Bones anxiously, "that you ought to put your feet in mustard and water, sir—awfully good tonic for a feller, sir. Bucks you up an' all that sort of thing, sir; uncle of mine who used to take too much to drink——"

"The only chance for me," said Hamilton, "is for you to clear out and leave me alone. Bones—quit fooling: I'm a sick man, and you've any amount of responsibility. Go up to the Isisi and watch things—it's pretty hard to say this to you, but I'm in your hands."

Bones said nothing.

He looked down at the fever-stricken man and thrust his hands in his pockets.

"You see, old Bones," said Hamilton, and now his friend heard the weariness and the weakness in his voice, "Sanders has a hold on these chaps that I haven't quite got . . . and . . . and . . . well, you haven't got at all. I don't want to hurt your feelings, but you're young, Bones, and these devils know how amiable you are."

"I'm an ass, sir," muttered Bones, shakily, "an' somehow

I understand that this is the time in my jolly old career when I oughtn't to be an ass . . . I'm sorry, sir."

Hamilton smiled up at him.

"It isn't for Sanders' sake or mine or your own, Bones—but for—well, for the whole crowd of us—white folk. You'll have to do your best, old man."

Bones took the other's hand, snivelled a bit despite his fierce effort of restraint, and went aboard the *Zaire*.

* * * * *

"Tell all men," said B'chumbiri, addressing his impassive relatives, "that I go to a great day and to many strange lands."

He was tall and knobby-kneed, spoke with a squeak at the end of his deeper sentences, and about his tired eyes he had twisted a wire so tightly that it all but cut the flesh: this was necessary, for B'chumbiri had a headache which never left him day or night.

Now he stood, his lank body wrapped in a blanket, and he looked with dull eyes from face to face.

"I see you," he said at last, and repeated his motto which had something to do with monkeys.

They watched him go down the street towards the beech where the easiest canoe in the village was moored.

"It is better if we go after him and put out his eyes," said his elder brother; "else who knows what damage he will do for which we must pay?"

Only B'chumbiri's mother looked after him with a mouth that drooped at the side, for he was her only son, all the others being by other wives of Mochimo.

His father and his uncle stood apart and whispered, and presently when, with a great waving of arms, B'chumbiri had embarked, they went out of the village by the forest path and ran tirelessly till they struck the river at its bend.

172

"Here we will wait," panted the uncle, "and when B'chumbiri comes we will call him to land, for he has the sickness *mongo*."

"What of Sandi?" asked the father, who was no gossip.

"Sandi is gone," replied the other, "and there is no law."

Presently B'chumbiri came sweeping round the bend, singing in his poor, cracked voice about a land and a people and treasures . . . he turned his canoe at his father's bidding, and came obediently to land. . . .

Overhead the sky was a vivid blue, and the water which moved quickly between the rocky channel of the Lower Isisi caught something of the blue, though the thick green of elephant grass by the water's edge and the overhanging spread of gum trees took away from the clarity of reflection.

There was, too, a gentle breeze and a pleasing absence of flies, so that a man might get under the red and striped awning of the *Zaire* and think or read or dream dreams, and find life a pleasant experience, and something to be thankful for.

Such a day does not often come upon the river, but if it does, the deep channel of the Isisi focuses all the joy of it. Here the river runs as straight as a canal for six miles, the current swifter and stronger between the guiding banks than elsewhere. There are rocks, charted and known, for the bed of the river undergoes no change, the swift waters carry no sands to choke the fairway, navigation is largely a matter of engine power and rule of thumb. Going slowly up stream a little more than two knots an hour, the *Zaire* was for once a pleasure steamer. Her long-barrelled Hotchkiss guns were hidden in their canvas jackets, the Maxims were lashed to the side of the bridge out of sight, and Lieutenant Augustus Tibbetts, who sprawled in a big wicker-work chair with an illustrated paper on his knees, a nasal-toned phonograph at his feet, and a long glass of lemon quash at his elbow, had little to do but pass the pleasant hours in the most pleasant occupation he could conceive, which was the posting of a diary, which he hoped on some future occasion to publish.

A shout, quick and sharp, brought him to his feet, a stiffly outstretched hand pointed to the waters.

"What the dooce——" demanded Bones indignantly, and looked over the side. . . . He saw the pitiful thing that rolled slowly in the swift current, and the homely face of Bones hardened.

"Damn," he said, and the wheel of the *Zaire* spun, and the little boat came broadside to the stream before the threshing wheel got purchase on the water.

It was Bones' sinewy hand that gripped the poor arm and brought the body to the side of the canoe into which he had jumped as the boat came round.

"Um," said Bones, seeing what he saw; "who knows this man?"

"Lord," said a wooding man, "this is B'chumbiri who was mad, and he lived in the village near by."

"There will we go," said Bones, very gravely.

. Now all the people of M'fa knew that the father of B'chumbiri and his uncle had put away the tiresome youth with his headache and his silly talk, and when there came news that the *Zaire* was beating her way to the village there was a hasty *likambo* of the elder men.

"Since this is neither Sandi nor M'ilitani who comes," said the chief, an old man, N'jela ("the Bringer"), "but Moon-in-the-Eye, who is a child, let us say that B'chumbiri fell into the water so that the crocodiles had him, and if he asks us who slew B'chumbiri—for it may be that he knows— let none speak, and afterwards we will tell M'ilitani that we did not understand him."

With this arrangement all agreed; for surely here was a palaver not to be feared.

174

Bones came with his escort of Houssas.

From the dark interiors of thatched huts men and women watched his thin figure going up the street, and laughed.

Nor did they laugh softly. Bones heard the chuckles of unseen people, divined that contempt, and his lips trembled. He felt an immense loneliness—all the weight of government was pressed down upon his head, it overwhelmed, it smothered him.

Yet he kept a tight hold upon himself, and by a supreme effort of will showed no sign of his perturbation.

The palaver was of little value to Bones; the village was blandly innocent of murder or knowledge of murder. More than this, all men stoutly swore that the thing that lay upon the foreshore for identification, surrounded by a crowd of frightened little boys lured by the very gruesomeness of the spectacle, was unknown, and laughed openly at the suggestion that it was B'chumbiri, who (said they) had gone a journey into the forest.

There was little short of open mockery and defiance when they pointed out certain indications that went to prove that this man was not of the Akasava, but of the higher Isisi.

So Bones' visit was fruitless.

He dismissed the palaver and walked back to his ship, and worked the river, village by village, with no more satisfactory result. That night in the little town of M'fa there was a dance and a jubilation to celebrate the cunning of a people who had outwitted and overawed the lords of the land, but the next day came Bosambo, who had established a system of espionage more far-reaching, and possibly more effective, than the service which the Government had instituted.

Liberties they might take with Bones; but they sat discomforted in palaver before this alien chief, swathed in monkey tails, his shield in one hand, and his bunch of spears in the other.

"All things I know," said Bosambo, when they told him what they had to tell, "and it has come to me that you have spoken lightly of Tibbetti, who is my friend and my master, and is well beloved of Sandi. Also they tell me that you smiled at him. Now I tell you there will come a day when you will not smile, and that day is near at hand."

"Lord," said the chief, "he made with us a foolish palaver, believing that we had put away B'chumbiri."

"And he shall return to that foolish palaver," said Bosambo grimly, "and if he goes away unsatisfied, behind I will come, and I will take your old men, and I will hang them by hooks into a tree and roast their feet. For if there is no Sandi and no law, behold I am Sandi and I law, doing the will of a certain bearded king, Togi-tani."

He left the village of M'fa a little unhappy for the space of a day, when, native-like, they forgot all that he had said.

In the meantime, up and down the river went Bones, palavers which lasted from sunrise to sunset being his portion.

He had in his mind one vital fact, that for the honour of his race and for the credit of his administration he must bring to justice the man who slew the thing which he had found in the river. Chiefs and elders met him with scarcely concealed scorn, and waited expectantly to hear his strong, foreign language. But in this they were disappointed, for Bones spoke nothing but the language of the river, and little of it.

He went on board the *Zaire* on the ninth night after his discovery, dispirited and sick at heart.

"It seems to me, Ahmet," he said to the Houssa sergeant who stood waiting silently by the table where his meagre dinner was laid, "that no man speaks the truth in this cursed land, and that they do not fear me as they fear Sandi."

"Lord, it is so," said Ahmet; "for, as your lordship knows, Sandi was very terrible, and then, O Tibbetti, he is an older man, very wise in the ways of these people, and very cunning to see their heart. All great trees grow slowly, O my lord! and that which springs up in a night dies in a day."

Bones pondered this for a while, then:

"Wake me at dawn," he said. "I go back to M'fa for the last palaver, and if this palaver be a bad one, be sure you shall not see my face again upon the river."

Bones spoke truly, his resignation, written in his sprawling hand, lay enveloped and sealed in his cabin ready for dispatch. He stopped his steamer at a village six miles from M'fa, and sent a party of Houssas to the village with a message.

The chief was to summon all elder-men, and all men responsible to the Government, the wearers of medals and the holders of rights, all landmen and leaders of hunters, the captains of spears, and the first headmen. Even to the witch-doctors he called together.

"O soldier!" said the chief, dubiously, "what happens to me if I do not obey his commands? For my men are weary, having hunted in the forest, and my chiefs do not like long palavers concerning law."

"That may be," said Ahmet, calmly. "But when my lord calls you to palaver you must obey, otherwise I take you, I and my strong men, to the Village of Irons, there to rest for a while to my lord's pleasure."

So the chief sent messengers and rattled his *lokali* to some purpose, bringing headmen and witch-doctors, little and great chiefs, and spearmen of quality, to squat about the palaver house on the little hill to the east of the village.

Bones came with an escort of four men. He walked slowly up the cut steps in the hillside and sat upon the stool to the chief's right; and no sooner had he seated himself than, without preliminary, he began to speak. And he spoke of Sanders, of his splendour and his power; of his love for all people and his land, and also M'ilitani, who these men respected because of his devilish blue eyes.

At first he spoke slowly, because he found a difficulty in breathing, and then as he found himself, grew more and more lucid and took a larger grasp of the language.

"Now," said he, "I come to you, being young in the service of the Government, and unworthy to tread in my lord Sandi's way. Yet I hold the laws in my two hands even as Sandi held them, for laws do not change with men, neither does the sun change whatever be the land upon which it shines. Now, I say to you and to all men, deliver to me the slayer of B'chumbiri that I may deal with him according to the law."

There was a dead silence, and Bones waited.

Then the silence grew into a whisper, from a whisper into a babble of suppressed talk, and finally somebody laughed. Bones stood up, for this was his supreme moment.

"Come out to me, O killer!" he said softly, "for who am I that I can injure you? Did I not hear some voice say *g'la*, and is not *g'la* the name of a fool? O, wise and brave men of the Akasava who sit there quietly, daring not so much as to lift a finger before one who is a fool!"

Again the silence fell. Bones, his helmet on the back of his head, his hands thrust into his pockets, came a little way down the hill towards the semi-circle of waiting eldermen.

"O, brave men!" he went on, "O, wonderful seeker of danger! Behold! I, *g'la*, a fool, stand before you and yet the killer of B'chumbiri sits trembling and will not rise before me, fearing my vengeance. Am I so terrible?"

His wide open eyes were fixed upon the uncle of B'chumbiri, and the old man returned the gaze defiantly.

"Am I so terrible?" Bones went on, gently. "Do men fear me when I walk? Or run to their huts at the sound of my puc-a-puc? Do women wring their hands when I pass?"

Again there was a little titter, but M'gobo, the uncle of B'chumbiri, grimacing now in his rage, was not among the laughters.

"Yet the brave one who slew——"

M'gobo sprang to his feet.

"Lord," he said harshly, "why do you put all men to shame for your sport?"

"This is no sport, M'gobo," answered Bones quickly. "This is a palaver, a killing palaver. Was it a woman who slew B'chumbiri? so that she is not present at this palaver. Lo, then I go to hold council with women!"

M'gobo's face was all distorted like a man stricken with paralysis.

"Tibbetti!" he said, "I slew B'chumbiri—according to custom—and I will answer to Sandi, who is a man, and understands such palavers."

"Think well," said Bones, deathly white, "think well, O man, before you say this."

"I killed him, O fool," said M'gobo loudly, "though his father turned woman at the last—with these hands I cut him, using two knives——"

"Damn you!" said Bones, and shot him dead.

*   *   *   *   *

Hamilton, so far convalescent that he could smoke a cigarette, heard the account without interruption.

"So there you are, sir," said Bones at the side. "An' I felt like a jolly old murderer, but, dear old officer, what was I to do?"

Still Hamilton said nothing, and Bones shifted uncomfortably.

"For goodness gracious sake don't sit there like a bally old owl," he said, fretfully. "Was I wrong?"

Hamilton smiled.

"You're a jolly old commissioner, sir," he mimicked. "and for two pins I'd mention you in dispatches."

Bones examined the piping of his khaki jacket and extracted the pins.

CHAPTER XII

THE MAN WHO DID NOT SLEEP

No doubt whatever but that Lieutenant Tibbetts of the Houssas had a pretty taste for romance. It led him to exercise latent powers of imagination and to garnish his voluminous correspondence with details of happenings which had no very solid foundation in fact.

On one occasion he had called down the heavy sarcasm of his superior officer by a reference to lions—a reference which Hamilton's sister had seen and, in the innocence of her heart, had referred to in a letter to her brother.

Whereupon Bones swore to himself that he would carefully avoid corresponding with any person who might have the remotest acquaintance with the remotest of Hamilton's relatives.

Every mail night Captain Hamilton underwent a cross-examination which at once baffled and annoyed him.

Picture a great room, the walls of varnished matchboarding, the bare floor covered in patches by skins. There are twelve windows covered with fine mesh wire and looking out to the broad verandah which runs round the bungalow. The furniture is mainly wicker work, a table or two bearing framed photographs (one has been cleared for the huge gramophone which Bones has introduced to the peaceful life of headquarters). There are no pictures on the walls save the inevitable five—Queen Victoria, King Edward, Queen Alexandra, and in a place of honour above the door the King and his Consort.

A great oil lamp hangs from the centre of the boarded ceiling, and under this the big solid table at either side of which two officers write silently and industriously, for the morrow brings the mail boat.

Silent until Bones looked up thoughtfully.

"Do you know the Gripps, of Beckstead, dear old fellow?"

"No."

"None of your people know 'em?" hopefully.

"No—how the dickens do I know?"

"Don't get chuffy, dear old chap."

Then would follow another silence, until—

"Do you happen to be acquainted with the Lomands of Fife?"

"No."

"I suppose none of your people know 'em?"

Hamilton would put down his pen, resignation on his face.

"I have never heard of the Lomands—unless you refer to the Loch Lomonds; nor to the best of my knowledge and belief are any of my relations in blood or in law in any way acquainted with them."

"Cheer oh!" said Bones, gratefully.

Another ten minutes, and then:

"You don't know the Adamses of Oxford, do you, sir?"

Hamilton, in the midst of his weekly report, chucked down his pen.

"No; nor the Eves of Cambridge, nor the Serpents of Eton, nor the Angels of Harrow."

"I suppose——" began Bones.

"Nor are my relations on speaking terms with them. They don't know the Adamses, nor the Cains, nor the Abels, nor the Moseses, nor the Noahs."

"That's all I wanted to know, sir," said an injured Bones. "There's no need to peeve, sir."

Step by step Bones was compiling a directory of people to whom he might write without restraint, providing he avoided mythical lion hunts and confined himself to anecdotes which were suggestively complimentary to himself.

Thus he wrote to one pal of his at Biggestow to the effect that he was known to the natives as "The-Man-Who-Never-Sleeps," meaning thereby that he was a most vigilant and relentless officer, and the recipients of this information, fired with a sort of local patriotism, sent the remarkable statement to the *Biggestow Herald and Observer and Hindhead Guardian*, thereby upsetting all Bones' artful calculations.

"What the devil does 'Man-Who-Never-Sleeps' mean?" asked a puzzled Hamilton.

"Dear old fellow," said Bones, incoherently, "don't let's discuss it. . . . I can't understand how these things get into the bally papers."

"If," said Hamilton, turning the cutting over in his hand, "if they called you 'The - Man - Who - Jaws - So - Much - That - Nobody - Can - Sleep,' I'd understand it, or if they called you 'The - Man - Who - Sleeps - With - His - Mouth - Open - Emitting - Hideous - Noises,' I could under stand it."

"The fact is, sir," said Bones, in a moment of inspiration, "I'm an awfully light sleeper—in fact, sir, I'm one of those chaps who can get along with a couple of hours' sleep—I can sleep anywhere at any time—dear old Wellin'ton was similarly gifted—in fact, sir, there are one or two points of resemblance between Wellington and I, which you might have noticed, sir."

"Speak no ill of the dead," reproved Hamilton; "beyond your eccentric noses I see no points of resemblance."

It was on a morning following the despatch of the mail that Hamilton took a turn along the firm sands to settle in his mind the problem of a certain Middle Island.

Middle Islands, that is to say the innumerable patches of land which sprinkle the river in its broad places, were a never-ending problem to Sanders and his successor. Upon these Middle Islands the dead were laid to rest—from the river you saw the graves with fluttering ragged flags of white cloth planted about them—and the right of burial was a matter of dispute when the mainland at one side of the river was Isisi land, and Akasava the other. Also some of the larger Middle Islands were colonised.

Hamilton had news of a coming palaver in relation to one of these.

Now, on the river, it is customary for all who desire inter-tribal palavers to announce their intention loudly and insistently. And if Sanders had no objection he made no move, if he did not think the palaver desirable he stopped it. It was a simple arrangement, and it worked.

Hamilton came back from his four-mile constitutional satisfied in his mind that the palaver should be held. Moreover, they had, on this occasion, asked permission. He could grant this with an easy mind, being due in the neighbourhood of the disputed territory in the course of a week.

It seemed that an Isisi fisherman had been spearing in Akasava waters, and had, moreover, settled, he and his family to the number of forty, on Akasava territory. Whereupon an Akasava fishing community, whose rights the intruder had violated, rose up in its wrath and beat Issmeri with sticks.

Then the king of the Isisi sent a messenger to the king of Akasava begging him to stay his hand "against my lawful people, for know this, Iberi, that I have a thousand spears and young men eager for fire."

And Iberi replied with marked unpleasantness that there were in the Akasava territory two thousand spears no less inclined to slaughter.

In a moment of admirable moderation, significant of the change which Mr. Commissioner Sanders had wrought in these warlike peoples, they accepted Hamilton's suggestion —sent by special envoy—and held a "small palaver," agreeing that the question of the disputed fishing ground should be settled by a third person.

And they chose Bosambo, paramount and magnificent chief of the Ochori, as arbitrator. Now, it was singularly unfortunate that the question was ever debatable. And yet it was, for the fishing ground in question was off one of the many Middle Islands. In this case the island was occupied by Akasava fishermen on the one shore and by the intruding Isisi on the other. If you can imagine a big "Y" and over it a little "o" and over that again an inverted "Y" thus "⅄" and drawing this you prolong the four prongs of the Y's, you have a rough idea of the topography of the place. To the left of the lower "Y" mark the word "Isisi," to the right the word "Akasava" until you reach a place where the two right hand prongs meet, and here you draw a line and call all above it "Ochori." The "o" in the centre is the middle island—set in a shallow lake through which the river (the stalk, of the Y's) runs.

Bosambo came down in state with ten canoes filled with counsellors and bodyguard. He camped on the disputed ground, and was met thereon by the chiefs affected.

"O, Iberi and T'lingi!" said he, as he stepped ashore, "I come in peace, bringing all my wonderful counsellors, that I may make you as brothers, for as you know I have a white man's way of knowing all their magic, and being a brother in blood to our Lord Tibbetti, Moon-in-the-Eye."

"This we know, Bosambo," said Iberi, looking askance at the size of Bosambo's retinue, "and my stomach is proud that you bring so vast an army of high men to us, for I see that you have brought rich food for them."

He saw nothing of the sort, but he wanted things made plain at the beginning.

"Lord Iberi," said Bosambo, loftily, "I bring no food, for that would have been shameful, and men would have said: 'Iberi is a mean man who starves the guests of his house.' But only one half of my wise people shall sit in your huts, Iberi, and the other half will rest with T'lingi of the Akasava, and feed according to law. And behold, chiefs and headmen, I am a very just man not to be turned this way or that by the giving of gifts or by kindness shown to my people. Yet my heart is so human and so filled with tenderness for my people, that I ask you not to feed them too richly or give them presents of beauty, lest my noble mind be influenced."

Whereupon his forces were divided, and each chief ransacked his land for delicacies to feed them.

It was a long palaver—too long for the chiefs.

Was the island Akasava or Isisi? Old men of either nation testified with oaths and swearings of death and other high matters that it was both.

From dawn to sunset Bosambo sat in the thatched palaver house, and on either side of him was a grass pot into which he tossed from time to time a grain of corn.

And every grain stood for a successful argument in favour of one or the other of the contestants—the pot to the right being for the Akasava, and that to the left for the Isisi.

And the night was given up to festivity, to the dancing of girls and the telling of stories and other noble exercises.

On the tenth day Iberi met T'lingi secretly.

"T'lingi," said Iberi, "it seems to me that this island is

not worth the keeping if we have to feast this thief Bosambo and search our lands for his pleasure."

"Lord Iberi," agreed his rival, "that is also in my mind —let us go to this robber of our food and say the palaver shall finish tomorrow, for I do not care whether the island is yours or mine if we can send Bosambo back to his land."

"You speak my mind," said Iberi, and on the morrow they were blunt to the point of rudeness.

Whereupon Bosambo delivered judgment.

"Many stories have been told," said he, "also many lies, and in my wisdom I cannot tell which is lie and which is truth. Moreover, the grains of corn are equal in each pot. Now, this I say, in the name of my uncle Sandi, and my brother Tibbetti (who is secretly married to my sister's cousin), that neither Akasava nor Isisi shall sit in this island for a hundred years."

"Lord, you are wise," said the Akasava chief, well satisfied, and Iberi was no less cheered, but asked: "Who shall keep this island free from Akasava or Isisi? For men may come and there will be other palavers and per-haps fighting?"

"That I have thought of," said Bosambo, "and so I will raise a village of my own people on this island, and put a guard of a hundred men—all this I will do because I love you both—the palaver is finished."

He rose in his stately way, and with his drums beating and the bright spearheads of his young men a-glitter in the evening sunlight, embarked in his ten canoes, having expanded his territory without loss to himself like the imperialist he was.

For two days the chiefs of the Akasava and the Isisi were satisfied with the justice of an award which robbed them both without giving an advantage to either. Then an uneasy realisation of their loss dawned upon them. Then followed a swift exchange of messages and Bosambo's colonisation scheme was unpleasantly checked.

Hamilton was on the little lake which is at the end of the N'gini River when he heard of the trouble, and from the high hills at the far end of the Lake sent a helio message staring and blinking across the waste.

Bones, fishing in the river below Ikan, picked up the instructions, and went flying up the river as fast as the new naphtha launch could carry him.

He arrived in time to cover the shattered remnants of Bosambo's fleet as they were being swept northward from whence they came.

Bones went inshore to the island, the water jacket of a Maxim gun exposed over the bow, but there was no opposition.

"What the dooce is all this about—hey?" demanded Lieutenant Tibbetts fiercely, and Iberi, doubly uneasy at the sound of an unaccustomed language, stood on one leg in his embarrassment.

"Lord, the thief Bosambo——" he began, and told the story.

"Lord," he concluded humbly, "I say all this though Bosambo is your relation since you have secretly married his sister's cousin."

Whereupon Bones went very red and stammered and spluttered in such a way that the chief knew for sure that Bosambo had spoken the truth.

Bones, as I have said before, was no fool. He confirmed Bosambo's order for the evacuation of the island, but left a Houssa guard to hold it.

Then he hurried north to the Ochori.

Bosambo formed his royal procession, but there was no occasion for it, for Bones was in no processional mood.

"What the dooce do you mean, sir?" demanded a glaring and threatening Bones, his helmet over his neck, his arms akimbo. "What do you mean, sir, by saying I'm married to your infernal aunt?"

"Sah," said Bosambo, virtuous and innocent, "I no savvy you—I no compreney, sah! You lib for my house—I give you fine t'ings. I make um moosic, sah——"

"You're a jolly old rotter, Bosambo!" said Bones, shaking his finger in the chief's face. "I could punish you awfully for telling wicked stories, Bosambo. I'm disgusted with you, I am indeed."

"Lord who never sleeps," began Bosambo, humbly.

"Hey?"

Bones stared at the other in amazement, suspicion, hope, and gratification in his face.

"O, Bosambo," said he mildly, and speaking in the native tongue, "why do you call me by that name?"

Now, Bosambo in his innocence had used a phrase (*M'wani-m'wani*) which signifies "the sleepless one," and also stands in the vernacular for "busy-body," or one who is eternally concerned with other people's business.

"Lord," said Bosambo, hastily, "by this name are you known from the mountains to the sea. Thus all men speak of you, saying: 'This is he who does not sleep but watches all the time.'"

Bones was impressed, he was flattered, and he ran his finger between the collar of his uniform jacket and his scraggy neck as one will do who is embarrassed by praise and would appear unconcerned under the ordeal.

"So men call me, Bosambo," said he carelessly, "though my lord M'ilitani does not know this—therefore in the day when M'ilitani comes, speak of me as *M'wani-m'wani* that he may know of whom men speak when they say 'the sleepless one.'"

Everybody knows that *Cala cala* great chiefs had stored against the hour of their need certain stocks of ivory.

Dead ivory it is called because it had been so long cut,

but good cow ivory, closer in grain than the bull elephant brought to the hunter, more turnable, and of greater value.

There is no middle island on the river about which some legend or buried treasure does not float.

Hamilton, hurrying forward to the support of his second-in-command, stopped long enough to interview two sulky chiefs.

"What palaver is this?" he demanded of Iberi, "that you carry your spears to a killing? For is not the river big enough for all, and are there no burying-places for your old men that you should fight so fiercely?"

"Lord," confessed Iberi, "upon that island is a treasure which has been hidden from the beginning of time, and that is the truth—N'Yango!"

Now, no man swears by his mother unless he is speaking straightly, and Hamilton understood.

"Never have I spoken of this to the Chief of the Isisi," Iberi went on, "nor he to me, yet we know because of certain wise sayings that the treasure stays and young men of our houses have searched very diligently though secretly. Also Bosambo knows, for he is a cunning man, and when we found he had put his warriors to the seeking we fought him, lord, for though the treasure may be Isisi or Akasava, of this I am sure it is not of the Ochori."

Hamilton came to the Ochori city to find a red-eyed Bones stalking majestically up and down the beach.

"What is the matter with you?" demanded Hamilton. "Fever?"

"Not at all," replied Bones, huskily; but with a fine carelessness.

"You look as if you hadn't had a sleep for months," said Hamilton.

Bones shrugged his shoulders.

"Dear old fellow," said he, "it isn't for nothing that I'm

called 'the sleepless one'—don't make sceptical noises, dear old officer, but pursue your inquiries among the indigenous natives, especially Bosambo—an hour is all I want—just a bit of a snooze and a bath and I'm bright an' vigilant."

"Take your hour," said Hamilton briefly. "You'll need it."

His interview with Bosambo was short and, for Bosambo, painful. Nevertheless he unbent in the end to give the chief a job after his heart.

Launch and steamer turned their noses down the stream, and at sunset came to the island. In the morning, Hamilton conducted a search which extended from shore to shore and he came upon the cairn unexpectedly after a two hours' search. He uncovered two tons of ivory, wrapped in rotten native cloth.

"There will be trouble over this," he said, thoughtfully, surveying the yellow tusks. "I'll go down stream to the Isisi and collect information, unless these beggars can establish their claim we will bag this lot for government."

He left Bones and one orderly on the island.

"I shall be gone two days," he said. "I must send the launch to bring Iberi to me; keep your eyes peeled."

"Sir," said Bones, blinking and suppressing a yawn with difficulty, "you can trust the sleepless one."

He had his tent pitched before the cairn, and in the shade of a great gum he seated himself in his canvas chair. . . . He looked up and struggled to his feet. He was half dead with weariness, for the whole of the previous night, while Bosambo snored in his hut, Bones, pinching himself, had wandered up and down the street of the city qualifying for his title.

Now, as he rose unsteadily to his feet, it was to confront Bosambo—Bosambo with four canoes grounded on the sandy beach of the island.

"Hello, Bosambo!" yawned Bones.

"O Sleepless One," said Bosambo humbly, "though I came in silence yet you heard me, and your bright eyes saw me in the little-light."

"Little-light" it was, for the sun had gone down.

"Go now, Bosambo," said Bones, "for it is not lawful that you should be here."

He looked around for Ahmet, his orderly, but Ahmet was snoring like a pig.

"Lord, that I know," said Bosambo, "yet I came because my heart is sad and I have sorrow in my stomach. For did I not say that you had married my aunt?"

"Now listen whilst I tell you the full story of my wickedness, and of my aunt who married a white lord——"

Bones sat down in his chair and laid back his head, listening with closed eyes.

"My aunt, O Sleepless One," began Bosambo, and Bones heard the story in fragments. ". . . Coast woman . . . great lord . . . fine drier of cloth. . . ."

Bosambo droned on in a monotonous tone, and Bones, open-mouthed, his head rolling from side to side, breathed regularly.

At a gesture from Bosambo, the man who sat in the canoe slipped lightly ashore. Bosambo pointed to the cairn, but he himself did not move, nor did he check his fluent narrative.

Working with feverish, fervent energy, the men of Bosambo's party loaded the great tusks in the canoes. At last all the work was finished and Bosambo rose.

*　　*　　*　　*　　*

"Wake up, Bones."

Lieutenant Tibbetts stumbled to his feet glaring and grimacing wildly.

"Parade all correct, sir," he said, "the mail boat has just come in, an' there's a jolly old salmon for supper."

"Wake up, you dreaming devil," said Hamilton.

Bones looked around. In the bright moonlight he saw the *Zaire* moored to the shelving beach, saw Hamilton, and turned his head to the empty cairn.

"Good Lord!" he gasped.

"O Sleepless One!" said Hamilton softly, "O bright eyes!"

Bones went blundering to the cairn, made a closer inspection, and came slowly back.

"There's only one thing for me to do, sir," he said, saluting. "As an officer an' a gentleman, I must blow my brains out."

"Brains!" said Hamilton scornfully.

*   *   *   *   *

"As a matter of fact I sent Bosambo to collect the ivory which I shall divide amongst the three chiefs—it's perished ivory, anyhow; and he had my written authority to take it, but being a born thief he preferred to steal it; you'll find it stacked in your cabin, Bones."

"In my cabin, sir!" said an indignant Bones; "there isn't room in my cabin, sir. How the dickens am I going to sleep?"

THE END